Tangle of Secrets

A Coming of Age Novel

Beverly Harris

RT Texan Press

Copyright © 2013 by Beverly Harris. All rights reserved.
No part of this book may be reproduced or transmitted in any form or by any means, electronic or mechanical, including photocopying, recording, or by any information storage and retrieval system, without permission in writing from the publisher.

Tangle of Secrets / by Beverly Harris

Printed in the United States of America
First Edition, July 2013

Cover illustration: © Julvil Dreamstime.com

For orders, contact:
Publisher: RT Texan Press, Clarewood House Box 911, Houston, TX, 77036.

Dedication

To my family, Michael, Jeffrey, and Amy, with all my love.

Contents

Dedication	i
1. For Carlos, wanting isn't getting	1
2. What was I thinking?	5
3. Bad advice from a hero	11
4. The piano, the police	15
5. Who was that visitor?	23
6. The backyard plot	31
7. Sneaking out to danger	35
8. Change of plans	43
9. Hurry, it's time to—what?	47
10. Nightmare in the archives	53
11. Escape in a daze	55
12. Writer vs. photographer	57
13. A dead man's desk	65

14. A cozy offer	71
15. Some rough spots	77
16. Togetherness, sort of	83
17. Ruined celebration	87
18. Bad news? No, the worst	97
19. No lovespeak	101
20. A need to know	105
21. Truth at last	109
22. Behind a door	121
23. Joyful confession	129
24. Arboreal solution	135
25. Getting real	139
26. A garden for choices	145
Acknowledgments	ii

1

For Carlos, wanting isn't getting

Our cab, honking and weaving toward the airport, was no place for an apology. To emphasize my culpability, Holly placed her carry-on bag between us and concentrated on her phone. I contained my guilt while she canceled and rescheduled interview appointments.

Tap, tap, tap—there was no let up.

Her preoccupation isolated me in simmering regret and a cloud of worry. If we missed the next flight to LA, I might be too late to see my father alive. Only a couple of hours ago I learned he'd been in a horrific car wreck.

Holly's trip, orchestrated by her uncle, was a surprise to both of us. While the timing was a huge puzzle to me, I was grateful she was along. She could calm me. Not immediately, though. After takeoff, I'd try again to rescue our promising relationship, meaning I'd have to convince her I'm not a certified jackass. That settled, I might have fortitude to face the family emergency.

My spark of hope went dark in a hurry. Last to board, we had to separate. I hoisted Holly's bag into the overhead and spotted the only other vacancy way down the aisle. I took the window seat after a struggle past two pairs of legs, the second belonging to a guy who spilled over both armrests.

Finally settled, I went over this morning's painful events, especially the conversation with my distraught mother. I had phoned her while chunking things into my backpack.

"Thank goodness you got my message, Carlos," she said. "Papa thinks he'll soon be with our Lord. He had a terrible, terrible wreck in that ugly old car." She sounded drained. "It hurts him to breathe. I'm so worried."

Hearing Mama crumble was weird. She always hid downside emotions behind closed doors.

My silent criticism, pointless under the circumstances, was that Pops would have edited her script from "ugly old car" to "magnificent vintage machine." In either case, it was now a pile of junk against a boulder on a San Bernadino mountainside. Pops was found only because a motorist, horrified at seeing him careen off the road, made an urgent call for help.

Pops was out of the intensive care unit and in a private room, awaiting further procedures. The medics predicted success, Mama said. Still, she feared the worst because his spirits were ebbing.

"Hurry," she said. "You need to be here right away. He has something to tell you—while he can still talk."

"Like what?"

She was quiet so long, I thought the call had dropped.

"It's not for me to say." She hesitated again. "You need to hear it from him."

***

From the air, I watched odd geometric lines—on otherwise barren land—slip beneath us. We were over a massive Texas gas field, a fascinating distraction from apprehension. An illustration in a nature studies book popped into my mind—a tangle of rattlesnakes under the sparse shade of a single desert bush. They could just as well be writhing in my chest.

For Carlos, wanting isn't getting

If Pops expected to die, he'd want to specify his final wishes, stuff about inheritance. I didn't want to hear it.

I've always loved the guy—except when I was a kid and strayed from his rules. His mighty discipline dramas terrified me. I blame Hollywood. Before cheap Westerns rode off into the sunset, Pops was a bit player. His youthful physique and Hispanic features adapted to the popular film stereotype of a shrieking Indian. All it took was savage makeup and daredevil horsemanship. The role must have appealed to him because, despite switching careers to commercial real estate, he never quit the warpath. No bloodshed. No swatting. He expressed authority over five kids solely with lightning in his eyes and thunder in his voice. I suspect my siblings dismissed those tirades as theatrical excess; for me, the youngest, each episode came across as final judgment with no chance of resurrection.

On the other hand, Pops spilled charm when adults were around. He liked to mess with ancient cars, swap jokes and insults over cards, and sing alto in a barbershop quartet. On free weekends and evenings back in my early days, he waltzed the family, minus one, out for concerts, shopping, games, and mountain sports.

I was the minus. I stayed home with a trusted caretaker.

When my complaints—over being left behind—pitched toward tantrums, Mama came up with a litany of excuses that came down to this: "You are too little, Baby. Your time will come."

Warm and maternal as she was to her kids' smallest needs and moods, she never guessed my mixed feelings. Part of me was glad to see them leave, especially my oldest brother Ricardo—make that Ricardo-the-Bully—who was a pain in the ear. Yes, ear. If he punched me, he'd catch hell, so he worked his damage by ridiculing my shortcomings.

He told me I didn't get to go along on outings because I wasn't part of the family. He said Mama found me abandoned in a dumpster with stinking garbage and dog poop.

His unforgivable words:

"You never belonged because you don't have brown eyes like the rest of us. Go look in the mirror, dummy."

True. Except for brownish yellow flecks, my eyes are mostly green. Ricardo's information gave them disturbing significance.

Then there was the alveolar trill, the fancy name for rolling r's in speech. As the son of third generation Americans, Emil and Irma Montero, I heard and understood occasional Spanish. So why was I the only one in the family (and general populace) who couldn't do the trill? Instead, I sprayed a mist of spit.

Ricardo pounced on that. He liked to sneak up from behind and yank my collar halfway down my spine just to hear a death rattle, which he considered a vocal improvement. Or, he mocked my speech defect by blowing loud and wet r-r-r-r-r-r's right into my ear.

A student encyclopedia in our home library gave me the news I needed. What a relief to read that green eyes, along with olive skin and dark hair, are not unheard of in the Mediterranean regions where my ancestors originated. Perfect. Ricardo-The-Jerk could expect revenge.

It amazes me even now to remember the destruction I caused.

2

What was I thinking?

Wandering passengers returned to their seats as a lunch cart inched down the plane's aisle. I ordered a Coke. Soon, eggy sandwich smells permeated the cabin and I adjusted the overhead airflow. Again, I gazed at the moving scenery, not really seeing anything, just mentally massaging my wounds.

I blamed my blow-up in front of Holly last evening on my parents' latest manipulation. No, it was more than that. It was not knowing—never knowing—their motives that finally set me off. I've always tried to ignore the gap in my personal information. Thinking about it raises uncomfortable questions, for which, by some unwritten code in the Montero family, answers are not forthcoming. Why the secrets, the smothering protection, all my life? Still fuming about my loss of control, I condensed my argument: I'm through with college. I'm 24 years old, and holding down a responsible job far from home. Is it asking too much to be treated as an adult?

All through childhood, I distanced my parents' perplexing behavior by blaming myself, too often with good reason. At age seven, I pulled everyone's chain with a memorable misdeed. And yeah, I messed up again soon afterward.

Tangle of Secrets

Back then, Mama had two quaint inspirations, two goals. First, she'd hire a hot portrait artist from Spain to paint each of us kids on our 16th birthdays. In nine years, she figured, he would have completed five large works. From upstairs, the long, glassed-in corridor overlooking the pool and Mama's landscaped garden invited their display. She'd have the coming-out party of the century.

Ricardo was the first to reach the magic age. His likeness, illuminated and tilted slightly forward, made dramatic viewing from ground level. Mama's contribution to the lofty scene was a bouquet of her prize-winning roses, a subtle echo of Ricardo's matching jacket. I had no interest in her micro-managed project, and cared little that she was already plotting the garden colors for Juanita, Alex, Carmela and me, in that order.

All I saw was a single, huge painting of my enemy.

Mama wasn't the only one with an inspiration. I had one, too.

Next time the family abandoned me for the crime of underage, I finished my dinner and homework at the kitchen table under watchful eyes of the cook, caretaker for the evening. I told her I'd be upstairs watching TV. In my room, I turned up the volume on *The Simpsons* and dug through my desk for artillery. Soon, with a box of indelible crayons in hand, I sneaked down the corridor to face that lone work of art. Ricardo smiled down at me as if he expected a trumpet fanfare and gifts of gold, incense, and myrrh.

I did have gifts: for starters, a black crayon.

His incisors were the first to receive. Presto: a bumpkin. I drew a long black handlebar mustache to form parentheses around his mouth. Soon he had circles of bright pink on his cheeks and a white bulbous clown nose. Next, his eyes. I was loving this—fiendish orange. With circular strokes, and by Ricardo's own rules, I banished him from the family.

Finally, in the lower right corner, I left my all-caps secret name, NONGENTI. It is Latin for 900, a fact I learned when my second

What was I thinking?

grade teacher got impatient with me for some reason and forced me to study Latin numerals. I saw a more important meaning to NON-GENTI that I kept secret.

To say my crayon expression caused an earthquake would be overestimating seismic power. This was way bigger. I could swear the whole house lifted off the ground and wobbled when my father roared. Mama, who loved Ricardo's portrait and recently had a preview party for her friends, muffled a scream against the back of her hand when she saw its hideous revision.

Ricardo slapped his own forehead and yelled "Shithead!" Several times. (I took his reaction as a victory.) Juanita, next in line to sit for the artist, and Carmela, 13, froze into statues with hands squeezed over their mouths. Alex, nearly 12, shook his head in miserable disappointment. That got to me, because Alex was my buddy.

With a mighty sweep of his arms, Pops shooed them away.

"Leave us alone," he said through tight lips.

He dug his fingers into my shoulder and guided me to the desk in my room. He pointed at the television.

"Turn that damn thing off."

I rushed to obey.

He sat on the edge of my bed and glared.

"Look me in the eye," he said. "Do I have your complete attention? Then listen to me. You—have—tested—my—patience. I don't know if I can control myself."

It looked like Armageddon for sure. I had seen him plenty angry. Never like this. It could only mean he was going to kill me without a single regret.

He aimed more word bullets through my forehead.

"What. In. God's. Name. Possessed. You?"

He expected an answer before he murdered me. With my thoughts squirming, a screwed-up scenario evolved.

"I tried to stop her, but she wouldn't listen."

Pops' back stiffened. "Who wouldn't listen?"

"The cook."

"The cook? Are you saying the cook ruined the portrait?"

I nodded. Ricardo was right—I was a shithead.

"All by herself?" Pops looked stunned.

"No. Not really."

"Then who else?"

"She asked Señor Hurtado to help her."

"I see. And why do you suppose the cook and the gardener would want to do such a thing?"

I fished in a swamp of lies and caught the dumbest.

"Because Ricardo teases them."

"Really! I didn't know that."

"He does it all the time."

"I had no idea." He studied me. "Has he ever teased you?"

Rats, a tactical error. He repeated, louder.

"Has he?"

Gazing at the floor, I nodded.

"What does he say to you?"

"Different things."

"Yes, but what does he say that upsets you most?"

My voice broke.

"He says I don't really belong to the family."

Pops pulled his chin back.

"Ridiculous. Why would he think that?"

"Because I'm the only one with green eyes."

Made vulnerable by confessing the wretched truth, my mind sent up a desperate prayer.

"Please don't let me cry."

The answer shot back straight from Heaven.

"Fat chance, shithead."

What was I thinking?

Pops' brow crinkled. He stared out of my balcony door. I could tell he was thinking about something he wouldn't share, a look I had seen many times before. When he faced me again, I witnessed a miracle. He appeared forgiving. Or, at least he had traded the fire in his eyes for a more reasonable troubled look.

"Ricardo will hear about that," he said. "He shouldn't be teasing the cook or the gardener either. They might get mad and quit, and then we wouldn't have anything for dinner and the weeds would grow right into the house, wouldn't they?"

His spontaneous imagery stunned me. I admired it.

"As for your green eyes—you got them from your mother's side of the family. They work just as well as brown ones, maybe better, understand? They are nothing to be ashamed of."

He checked his watch and growled.

"It's way past your bedtime."

To my amazement, he dropped the inquisition and stood to leave. I was alive.

At the door, he turned back to fling another dark look. The least I expected was the cruelest of all punishments—that I apologize to Ricardo.

"Son, you are very special in this family," Pops said. "But I'm concerned about your tendency to fabricate stories. Keep it up and you'll turn into a godforsaken screenwriter."

Despite Pops' apparent pardon, and his use of the word "fabricate" which I'd have to look up, the unfortunate episode left me feeling further estranged from the family. Parental consultations behind closed doors multiplied.

I stood apart in a funk the next day when Mama said she telephoned the Madrid artist. He agreed to come back, repair his work and, while he was here, get started on Juanita's portrait. Mama seemed content with that, but by her sideways glances at me, I detected an undercurrent of disbelief and worry about my destructive conduct.

    Shame lingered. The experience told me to consider consequences before I acted. Trouble was, the lesson didn't sink in before I screwed up again.

3

Bad advice from a hero

The airline's excuse for a seat got smaller, shorter, or maybe my muscles only reflected the turmoil in my head. I told my fellow passengers I needed to get up. They struggled upward to let me squeeze by. Once unfolded in the aisle, I debated about checking Holly's mood. I could see her. She was asleep. Her hair tumbled over one soft cheek toward lips that aroused a memory of our one brief kiss and its promise of fireworks to come.

Though only a few steps away, I sensed we were miles apart. I retreated to the lavatory.

After making my way back to my seat, I wanted to doze like Holly, get some rest for the ordeal ahead. Instead, my mind droned on about my relationship with Pops. Was it all my imagination that he treated me differently from my siblings? A touch of caution, maybe? Never either solid disapproval or genuine affection? I really didn't know the answers, even though many a time I wondered how he really felt about a painful incident that changed my life.

***

Two consuming pastimes and one passionate hobby owned me as a kid. I was nuts about bugs and photography. Almost any free daylight hour found me in Mama's lush garden aiming a lens at insects in their natural settings. Many gave up their lives, moving from collection jars to slides for macro shots or for mounting on Styrofoam.

Juanita and Carmela agreed they'd rather swallow mugs of slime than enter my creepy room. Good thing. That meant tattletale sisters would also keep out of my journal where I detailed photo settings and stinging opinions about the family.

My hobby? Super hero comic books. Stacks of them.

Another thing. I had an imagination that swept me like cosmic dust into a fantasy world. People would ask why I was staring at them. News to me, because I'd be so caught up in an alternate life that real people disappeared.

Super Big Guy, Interplanetary Man of Muscle, was my best friend. He stepped out of comic book pages to help me perform amazing deeds. He appeared only when I was alone, never at school or the dinner table. He showed me how to snorkel in the shallow end of the pool. He helped me spot insects and work out camera settings. He convinced me that, if I applied myself, some day I could be a real photographer, maybe at a newspaper with exciting assignments.

Soon after the portrait incident, he noticed that I needed cheering up.

"Tell you what, Boy," he said. "How would you like to fly like me? I'll teach you to soar off your balcony way up over the city. Okay?"

Leave it to Super Big Guy to come up with a thriller. He stood like an alien deity on the balcony rail, his cape flapping in the Pacific breeze. I took his hand and let him pull me up beside him.

He said we'd get airborne with one mighty shove and rise above the green gem ficus tree that reached for the balcony. We'd swoop over the stone wall. Like magnificent birds, we'd soar far above the LA smog.

Observing my moves, my hero gave me the ultimate compliment.

Bad advice from a hero

"Excellent form, young man. Now let's fly."

In unison, we shouted "Blast off!"

I don't know the direction Super Big Guy went. I crashed though the tree and smacked down on the path below. Half an hour later, Mama and Pops found me broken, bloodied and incoherent. I was alive thanks only to bushy branches that slowed my fall.

Machine bleeps and fuzzy babble defined my next three weeks. Only one image focused through the confusion. When Mama left my side for a few minutes, probably to grab a sandwich, a mean nurse wearing a hospital mask came into my room. She pulled me out of bed into a wheelchair. She struggled and nearly dropped me. My broken ankle twisted and I cried out in agony. The next moment she let go and rushed out of the room—at the same time Mama flew in. My voice shaking, I tried to describe what happened. Mama looked plenty troubled. Caressing my brow, she insisted that everything was all right, that it had only been a scary nightmare. I didn't believe her. I could still feel throbbing where the nurse had grabbed me and I remembered her pressing voice saying, "Carlos, come with me. Hurry."

* * *

After finishing a long vigil by my hospital bed one evening, Pops went home to bolt the balcony door. My secret journal lay on the desk. Apparently he was unimpressed by the cover where I had scrawled in scarlet crayon: "Private. Keep Out or Die."

He read it. Behind pages of elementary insect and plant science, I had noted my extreme frustrations with the family. I complained about each sibling: Ricardo was a snake, Juanita ignored me, Alex was too busy. Carmela and her friends were all snobs. The cook and the gardener were mean. Mama was impatient and cared more for her plants than for me. Pops hated me.

I still have the journal, which, from an adult perspective, only reflects a youngest child's unreasonable plea for constant attention. Pops had a different interpretation. He convinced Mama that I was depressed and had tried to commit suicide. Together they plotted a regimen to fill every hour of my life, which forever after excluded Super Big Guy.

I learned of their actions after my concerned parents handed me to a psychiatrist every Saturday morning, hoping to restore my mental health before I harmed the family. They enrolled me in gentle activities: piano, nature club, library reading program, and advanced camera study with a gift of new lenses and a tripod. As my bones firmed up, they found more active pursuits: diving, skiing and scouting. In all situations, a watchful adult stood nearby.

Something else surfaced. Alex-the-Detective confided he eavesdropped on a conversation Mama and Pops had in their bedroom. With his keen investigative ear to the door, he heard them mention my name and talk about kidnapping. I was dumbfounded. Why me?

"You're the smallest, the easiest to pick off," he said, neglecting to speculate on motive.

A connection dawned between his news and my "nightmare" at the hospital. I told Alex about the mean nurse. His eyes widened. If I swore not to tell, he said, he'd share some more secrets. I took the oath.

He had noticed a guy on our property.

"I drilled him," Alex said. "His name is Humberto. Pops hired him as a night security guard. He's an ex-cop, licensed to pack heat. Guns."

I had seen enough TV cop shows to know the circumstances of kidnapping, and understood that often the victim was found dead. Abandonment wasn't my biggest concern any more. Now it was threats from outside and suffocating control from inside. These weren't temporary conditions. They lingered for years. So if Pops in his present suffering had something to tell me now, let it be what I wanted to know.

4

The piano, the police

The plane moved out of New Mexico. Arizona's vast desert had decorated itself with a welcoming double rainbow, the ends visible from my loft. No pots of gold. So help me, I looked—anything for diversion. I would have dozed off but for the rhythmic snoring of the passenger in the adjoining seat.

I rewound back to childhood and Alex. After alerting me to my possible doom, he offered a remedy.

"Humberto won't let anything bad happen. He's a Sensei," he said. "A master in karate. He said he'll teach you self-defense and I asked if I could join in. He said sure, and the girls could too."

During the lessons, Humberto seemed ancient to me. In his late forties, he flashed mighty muscles. Even his eyebrows bulged when he anticipated a move. Yet there was gentleness about him. I noticed it when he gauged my strength and range of movements to make sure I had recovered enough for the rigors of martial arts.

Soon we kids were testing our skills around the house, grabbing, chopping, and knocking over chairs, yelling ee-YAH! I gained respect for my oldest sister. Although Juanita looked as delicate as the first strand of a cobweb, she could flatten a guy in a second. I hoped she'd be along if I got kidnapped. Carmela, on the intersection of teen-age angst and cluelessness, lost interest after the first lesson and announced that the stiff white karate uniform was ugly and she wouldn't wear it to a pig's funeral. Humberto, ex-cop that he was, took offense at the pig reference. He rolled his eyes and with strained politeness told her she was free to go shopping.

My reward came when I learned I could cripple Ricardo-the-Jerk. In private, Humberto showed me how a small person can overtake a large one. When he thought I was ready, he invited Ricardo to volunteer as my adversary. With a smirk, Ricardo asked if it's lawful to mangle a pipsqueak.

I didn't wait for an answer. I ee-YAHed him flat to the floor. He landed funny and dislocated his pinkie, so I got no accolades—other than the multitude I bestowed on myself.

While karate was fun and useful, another of my parents' therapeutic goals had a terrifying and far-reaching result. In all of their careful plans for my mental health and safety from sinister forces, they never dreamed that innocent piano lessons could turn into a matter for the police.

Had I understood the depth of their fears, I might have curbed my imagination. At the psychiatrist's I wouldn't have insisted that Pops locked me in the freezer every night. I wouldn't have reported sighting Mary Mother of God at a Big Bear ski slope. And at piano class, I might have stopped playing when the instructor talked, and quit talking when he asked me to play.

He was a shaky old guy, chosen after Pops checked his reputation as a musician and head of a music academy. Right off, my motor mouth exasperated him.

Several futile lessons later the master fired himself and turned me over to a new employee, a twenty-something instructor who called himself Angkor What (his misspelling of Angkor Wat, an ancient Cambodian temple). The guy, whose light hair looked like

The piano, the police

a fuzzy umbrella, identified himself as a front man for a gig-playing rock band, the What Nexus.

At our first session, he watched me in combat with printed music. I'd take my fingers off the keyboard and jab at a note I couldn't name. Too often the sheet of music flipped off the rack and I'd have to slide from the bench to retrieve it. Finally Angkor shook his mound of hair and murmured.

"Just let yourself go, man. Skip the brain stuff. Let the music flow from your heart place." He played a few Calypso riffs on his guitar to match my endeavor and grunted something that sounded like, *"Me and you...me and you, looking for greenness bending around a corner, oh yeah..."* He caught my attention with a nod toward the piano.

Hey, cool. It worked. There it was, music happening all over the keyboard. More important than feeling the music, I felt his approval.

"You got rhythm, man," he said. "You ought to get you some bongos."

For a change, Mama and Pops hadn't paid full attention because they weren't aware of the teacher switch, that I'd been put in the hands of a rocker who smelled like refinery waste. But I immediately recognized a hero when I saw one.

When he asked me if I'd like to see the studio where rockers practice and hang out, I got so carried away with the prospect, I forgot my obligation to be at the front door when Pops arrived to pick me up.

So I wasn't there.

Oh, man.

I can imagine how Pops reacted to the news. He would have accused the academy of committing a major infraction of their contract. Pops' roar would leave the terrified old music teacher with barely enough breath to guess where Angkor might be.

17

Meanwhile, I was having a captivating experience, unconcerned that Angkor and I had left the premises without permission. I expected the studio to be a relic to match the gray, run-down surroundings we drove past, but not so—the flat brick building looked brand new. Inside, Angkor pointed out a warren of sound-proofed compartments. I counted 40 of them while we waited at the desk of a pretty clerk. She sat near the entrance collecting fees from musicians who hugged a variety of instruments. Angkor reached into his pocket.

"Hey, babe, what's in the ice chest today? Got a drink for the prodigy here?"

He gave her a bill, disappeared into an anteroom behind her desk, and emerged with an opened bottle of cold orangeade. I didn't want to complain to my new hero, but I hate phony orange stuff. One swallow and yuk. Since he was giving me an expectant look, I forced another swallow. Double yuk.

We stood for a while with several musicians who exchanged news about gigs. I had trouble understanding their jargon because nobody seemed to finish a sentence—another trait to admire. They were about to move to individual practice rooms when the front door flew open.

Four police officers burst in.

The meanest looking officer swept cold eyes over the group and settled on me.

"What's your name, son?"

"Carlos."

"Carlos Montero?"

I nodded.

"Okay. Where's your piano teacher?"

I glanced at Angkor. I could swear his hair drooped like a scolded dog's ears.

"You his teacher?" asked a different cop.

"I am. What's the problem?"

The piano, the police

A police officer pulled me close and took the orange drink out of my hands while his partner, gun drawn, approached Angkor.

"Raise your hands high and turn around," the first cop said, and did a quick pat-down and checked Angkor's driver's license. There was a quick interrogation about Angkor's vehicle and one of the officers went back outside.

The musicians and I stood frozen, breathing through our mouths. The clerk, her eyelids fluttering, started to raise her telephone, but thought better of it.

I was fascinated by police details, how Angkor was told to drop to his knees with feet crossed in back and to place his hands, fingers entwined, over his head. Handcuffs fastened over one wrist, then the other. A female in plain clothes appeared. She'd been talking on a police radio.

She faced Angkor and spoke in a throaty, intolerant tone:

"Sir, you are under arrest for the unlawful removal of a juvenile."

As "my" officer led me outside, I wanted to ask a million questions. Where were we going? To jail? What would happen to Angkor? I'd tell everybody he was really a nice guy, that he did not kidnap me. But by the time I was placed in an unmarked car, I didn't feel like talking. My vision started to blur.

The officer introduced me to the woman with the tense voice and radio.

"Son, this is Detective Willis. She'll stay with you until the ambulance gets here."

A deep-seated dread churned up. Why an ambulance? I didn't fall off the balcony or out of a tree. I was just starting to have fun.

I turned to see Angkor. Policemen on either side of him were making him walk backward toward a patrol car. Angkor had parked his old car three spaces down. A different officer was training a flashlight inside.

Detective Willis sat beside me on the front seat.

"How do you feel, Carlos?" She sounded a lot softer, more like a mother.

I wasn't sure how to describe my fuzzy feelings and a growing ache in the back of my head, so I didn't try. Instead, I asked her to let me use her phone to call my parents.

"Hon, this isn't a phone, it's a recorder. My supervisor already called your parents. They're at the Police Bureau. They'll be at the hospital when you get there."

I remember hearing her ask, "Carlos, do you want to tell me anything? Did…"

A siren drowned out her voice. As it approached, it faded, and so did I.

Had I been kidnapped? Or was the incident a mere lapse in judgment? I learned later it didn't matter to the cops. Their on-the-spot check showed Angkor What had a record as a drug dealer. That beam from the cop's flashlight settled some years of his future by illuminating a stash of cocaine and drug paraphernalia.

Except for the discomfort of a rapid pulse, puffy lips, and a rash, I enjoyed special concern from my parents. It ended with a call from the hospital. The result of my tests showed no evidence of narcotics. My discomfort resulted from my yuk factor, an acute allergy to citrus food dye.

According to Alex (I should write a book by that name), Pops had raged that my orange drink had been doped and suspected "the hippie freak" had been hired. By whom? Silence. Alex observed that Pops shut down after the lab report.

"Like when people realize they've said too much," Alex decided.

**

As Mama had predicted, in due time I passed the "not too little any more" test and was allowed to join the family, minus two, on outings. Ricardo and Juanita, away in college, were the minuses. If

The piano, the police

I experienced a turning point in those years, it was at USC football games—not so much the game as the halftimes when the incredible Trojan drumline performed. It was like watching a row of Super Big Guys with acute timing, a human machine that drove all the birds out of the neighborhood. I was hooked. I schemed for a drum set, begging to trade Scout meetings for percussion lessons.

Mama accepted the idea, which she saw as another handy way to keep me at home. She had the music room soundproofed and let me invite guys over to make up a band. I wasn't allowed to go to their houses, though, because she didn't know their parents. They might be too lenient and let us take off for god-knows-where.

I was lectured often and at length. My parents never caught on that their rules were influencing me to hatch devious plans in my teen years when reckless courage caught up with my lust for freedom.

5

Who was that visitor?

I was 14 when Mama unintentionally put me in harm's way. She signed me up for a church-sponsored day camp in the Santa Monica Mountains. I groaned when the announcement appeared in the church bulletin, stating that an "experienced nature photographer" would teach.

"I told the camp counselor how good you are taking pictures," she said. "Each camper will have a small camera. Okay?"

Well, that was different. It might be neat to face an attentive young audience with bright questions, the way it was at a USC photo workshop I had attended. I figured I knew most of the answers. To acknowledge my stirring hormones, if I impressed a couple of cool chicks, so be it.

She drove me to the campsite early that morning and helped unload my gear. The aim would be to use only natural light and capture denizens of the woods, meaning in Southern California elevations squirrels, raccoons, foxes, quail, butterflies, and if we were unlucky, black bears.

A few minutes later, a church bus roared up. Its door squawked open and out poured two dozen screaming six-year-olds. I had been sabotaged by my own mother. She chatted briefly with the two leaders, then headed back down the mountain to her garden club meeting. I would have enjoyed a sulk if not for my immediate need for survival. The head counselor and bus driver, Joanna, acted satisfied just to be alive after unloading supplies. She stretched out on a bedroll with a paperback novel. Her co-counselor, Sandra, mother of twins Kip and Taylor, barked orders at the racket. Just when the noise level dropped, Kip and Taylor got into it. Kip stamped her foot and yelled at him, "Don't say any more words to me!" Sandra gave me a look.

"Do something," she said.

I took that to mean quit staring at the chaos and take charge. Dim memories of a scout leader surfaced. He may have been on the edge of a breakdown, yet his system for getting attention worked.

"Okay, guys," I shouted. "Okay, guys," I shouted again. "Get in a line and follow me. I want to hear you yelling and whooping like Apaches. We're going to do an Indian war dance." Using my backpack as a tom-tom, I invented a step that would mortify a real Indian, but the kids, limbs flying, gave it their all. Dancing in an ever tighter circle, I had them halt, drop their little butts to the ground, and listen. It was time for a photography lesson, beginning with shutters.

"When you push this button, hold your breath," I said. "That way, you won't move and your picture will be sharp."

A hand went up.

"Will it cut me?"

An enduring lesson for me: Speak the language of your audience.

My inspiring lecture finished, and with Sandra trailing, I led the determined team through mid-morning sunlight to the edge of a thicket. We paused at an interesting rock formation. Clickety-clickety-click. We turned over a medium-sized log to see what would crawl out. Screams. We found a bird's nest. "Aw-w-w." My brain skipped back and forth from vigilance for the group to spotting novel photo possibilities.

Who was that visitor?

At one point, we had to separate boys from girls and take each group deeper behind some trees for nature's call. I don't know how the girls carried on, but the boys started shooting naughty pictures of each other's exposures. My lessons two and three: Expect anything, and show the boys how to delete shots from their cameras before parental inspection.

Somehow, we got back to camp with only a few scratches. Hearing the approaching army, Joanna unwrapped sandwiches, vinegary pickles and mellow cheeses, our awards for a job well done; I mean, we hadn't lost anyone and the kids were newly educated, weren't they?

Not exactly. A pouty little girl named Coquita planted herself on the ground nearby. When asked to come to the table, she pivoted away from us. We heard a pitiful "mew" sound that could not be ignored. Sandra leaned over her.

"Sweetheart, what's the matter? Why are you so sad?"

"I feel sorry for the pretty trees."

To her credit, Sandra showed deep concern.

"Why, Coquita?"

"Because they can't see each other."

It was Sandra's turn to look pitiful. With a glance, she invited me to solve the problem.

"I took Coquita's clammy hand and guided her a few feet away to a nearby black oak whose tall branches danced in the breeze.

"You're right," I told her. "The trees can't see, but their leaves sure can talk to each other. Listen. Hear all that rustling?"

She nodded.

"Know what? They whisper to each other all night long."

She needed proof.

"What do they say?"

"They're saying it's time to drop their acorns."

"Why?"

I answered with squeaky cartoon voices of an imaginary mouse, deer and dove. Each character drooled over the idea of munching on delicious acorns, even as leftovers buried for later.

"Coquita, how'd you like to bury your peanut butter and jelly sandwich for later?"

"Eeewww."

"Right. But guess what magic can happen to a buried acorn."

"What?"

"It can grow up into a tree."

"And will it whisper?"

"Right, girl. You're so quick."

Fantasy danced in her eyes as she gazed upward at swaying branches. She had entered my world of make-believe where lessons are disguised as play. I was there too, thinking how this child could learn from my hoard of nature pictures. So much to learn and a great age to soak it all up. Maybe I should suggest a class...

Clamor at the picnic table rattled our daydreams.

"Coquita, the squirrels aren't the only ones who get hungry. We're hungry too, aren't we?"

"No, I'm starving!"

"You're starving? I thought you were Coquita."

She perched hands on hips to scold.

"You're so silly!"

We must have looked pleased with ourselves because Joanna sensed the problem was solved.

"Drinks coming up," she called.

She made an abrupt turn toward a nearby noise.

A car, crunching leaves and twigs, pulled into sight. It stopped alongside the church bus.

"Who's that?" asked Sandra.

"No idea," Joanna said. "Carlos, go see. If they're friendly, invite them over. If not, threaten 'em with your sharp pictures."

Who was that visitor?

I approached the driver just as she rolled down her window. She was alone. She had smooth olive skin, a precise cut of black hair, no makeup, and aviator shades. Her face lit up with a friendly smile.

"Hi," she said. "I read the church bulletin about your day camp. I thought I'd be a Good Samaritan and donate some yummies. You must be Carlos, right?"

"I am. And you?"

"Here," she said, handing me a sizeable box. "It's full of chocolate-flavored energy bars."

I thanked her, not without misgivings. We needed more energy around here like we needed more cameras.

"The notice said you're teaching photography. You must be a very smart young man. Good camera work is complicated."

"Not when you get the hang of it."

She tilted her head in a searching way.

"It's pretty up here," she said. "Did you get some good shots?"

"Yeah. The kids are fast learners."

"I could use a little help myself." She reached into her handbag and pulled out, of all things, another drugstore camera. "It's new. Do I need to know anything special?"

I gave her the same instructions I had given the kids.

Looking eager to experiment, she aimed the camera at me. She clicked and checked the image on the small LCD screen.

"Hey, not bad. You're a good-looking subject."

She took a deep breath as if to reward herself by inhaling the woods.

"Outings like this are so healthy for children, aren't they? Especially if they have a leader who encourages imagination."

With the conversation going nowhere, I suggested, "Come on over. We have plenty of sandwiches."

"Oh, thanks, but I have to get back."

From the way she hesitated, I got the feeling something was

left unsaid, but finally she added, "It was nice meeting you, Carlos."

"Thanks."

"Well, goodbye."

I watched her ease the car around and crunch back down the mountain. The sound of her voice, warm but oddly guarded, lingered.

"Who was it?" said Joanna when I handed her the energy bars.

"I don't know."

"You didn't ask?"

"I did, but she didn't answer."

"That's odd."

"Yeah. I guess it is."

***

Mama was waiting when the bus pulled into the church's back parking lot.

"How was it?"

"How was what?"

"Never mind. I can see you're tired."

She helped load my never-used stuff into the back seat. City traffic was a purr after grinding down the mountain in a bus loaded with noisy seat-kickers. After a few blocks, I revived enough to answer her question—and surprised myself.

"It was interesting. Kind of fun," I said.

The camp had been my first exposure to teaching, at developing a nature curriculum, and dealing with mercurial little kids. Until now, the little kid had always been me. The experience left me with an unexpected sense of fulfillment and a hint of possibilities—interactive nature books, maybe, to inspire more little Coquitas. I could picture her touching a button to hear the illustrated pages answer her questions or show a video with the sounds of creatures. And whispering trees.

Who was that visitor?

Mama used my positive response as a gate to a dozen more questions. I had one of my own:

"Is there a woman in church, maybe in her early thirties, nice-looking for her age?"

"That's not much to go on. *Latina?*"

"Yeah, probably."

"What's her name?"

"I'm asking you. She showed up at camp around noon and brought some snacks for the kids. But she left in big hurry and didn't introduce herself."

"That's odd. She didn't talk to anybody?"

"Just me. She knew my name, said she read about the day camp and me in the church bulletin."

"But your name wasn't..." Mama's voice changed to a whisper. "It just said an experienced nature photographer." The way she tightened her hands on the steering wheel, I could tell she was concentrating on more than the traffic.

"Yeah, I noticed that. You talked me into teaching because you said it was already in the bulletin, but it wasn't. I mean, the day camp notice was, but not my name. Why?"

"You might have backed out. And I'd have to explain your actions."

"No fair. You're sneaky. So do you know that lady?"

Mama shook her head. The twice-stated question made her uncomfortable. I helped her out by changing the subject.

"Is Pops home?"

"Hmm? Oh, he should be by now. The Quartet went to Orange County for a music festival."

We pulled into our driveway. Pops, still in his barber costume, stood at the door in a jaunty pose, one hand leaning against the frame, the other holding a brandy. On purpose, his paste-on handlebar mustache clung lop-sided to his upper lip. When Mama approached him,

29

he widened his eyes and extended his arms, brandy included, in a vaudevillian show of desperate passion. He grabbed her, crushed her against his body and sang hotly into her face:

"Let me call you sweetheart, I'm in love with you. Let me hear you whisper that you love me too-o-o."

He caught his breath and continued *"...o-o-o-o-o."*

At that ridiculous point Mama did whisper into his ear. For a minute I thought she was going along with his goofiness, but her words shattered his mood. His tone plunged.

"I see," he said under his breath. He didn't notice when his mustache fell to the floor.

I went to the kitchen to negotiate with the cook. It had been a long day on the edge of civilization and I felt malnourished. Mama and Pops, looking grim, went to their room and closed the door.

6

The backyard plot

When I turned 16, I put my camera on a tripod, arranged lights, and set a timer for taking a picture of myself. I offered the printed result to the Spanish artist when he arrived to do my portrait. I explained in Spanglish and spittle that, by using the photo, he could paint without a live subject. His live subject, meanwhile, could take off with brother Alex for a session of racquetball at the gym.

It turned out that Mama got wind of the plan. Enough said. She made me put on a shirt the color of a yellow daffodil and told me to sit. I sat. And sat.

The Madrid artist's final stroke of brush alerted Mama to go nuts with party plans. Not only did she invite the usual adult roster, she asked each of us for a list of our friends.

"Tell them to bring their bathing suits," she said. "I'm hiring mariachis. Emilio, get someone to hang the Christmas lights and piñatas, and what else?" She mentioned keeping things simple, then immediately planned a buffet of guisada, beef fajitas, arroz con pollo, chicken mole, tamales, potato salad, and sausages. Pops reeled under the barrage of chatter.

"Irma," he begged, "instead of all this Mexican merriment, couldn't we have a stuffy English tea dance instead?"

She dismissed his joke with a killer look, and went right on: "I'm going to call the caterer and the party store. We'll need to set up tables, and I'll want them to make up bunches of paper flowers. Lots of them."

She had the gardener relocate a bulk of potted plumeria and exotic hibiscus to make more room near the pool.

The party happened. A blast from mariachis at the far end of the setting signaled guests to stream outside into Mama's high-budget replica of a fiesta. Squealing kids raced past tall legs for the water. Adults, margaritas in hand, turned up their volume to make party talk. There was shoulder-slapping by the men, cooing by older women. Several aunts informed me that I had grown—how do you answer stuff like that? Young adults—that would include my sisters and their friends—flitted in and out of the house. Juanita introduced her latest boyfriend, Danny, a congenial chef she met at a cooking lesson. Ricardo and his new wife, Judith, made a brief appearance, just long enough to give Mama the impression that glamorous Judith may have imbibed before she arrived. To further Mama's consternation, my friends and I split to the far reaches of the back yard between a stand of bamboo and citrus trees where we exercised our specialties of brood and mumble.

Pops' tolerance for traditional music soon hit its limit. Using cagey diplomacy, he signaled the players to rest their instruments and form a line at the flower-dripping, sizzling buffet. Mama captured the lull with a little speech to introduce the guest of honor, the Madrid artist. The climax of the evening was then at hand, she said, and invited everyone to gaze upward at the corridor of portraits. One by one, the paintings and companion bouquets debuted in a beam of light.

Whistles and applause.

The backyard plot

When the final spotlight revealed my impatient expression hardened in oils, unrefined noises from my friends cut through polite applause.

Our leader was a hulky classmate we named Zonko. He claimed to be the nephew of a porn star. He once asked me to edit his English paper, which started "Because I have no memory of being born, there is strong reason to believe it never happened."

Hardly a phantom, he swaggered behind a startling black beard. When Mama got her first look at him, her backbone slipped a notch.

Zonko vowed he had been with dozens of women. We were fascinated, even though experience indicated he felt no obligation to facts. What he did have was street experience and powerful persuasion. Out of his wayward brain came the notion that our coterie needed to make a secret excursion to forbidden haunts. It would have to begin late one night when I could crawl over the balcony rail, climb down the ficus tree and elude Humberto, our steadfast night security guard. With careful timing, my friends, all with their brains set in reverse, would be waiting in a car outside our wall.

7

Sneaking out to danger

By age 16, I'd been exposed to the wiles of the wealthy, to the elite of talent, to upper crust schooling and recreation, but never to urban wisdom. For that, Los Angeles is a colorful classroom. It offers extremes, from glitz to god-awful, grand to gritty. Before treading in certain neighborhoods, the explorer had better know who owns which sidewalk.

While I didn't want a drastic challenge, some street smarts and the chance to experiment with stuff would be cool, if not required. At this stage of my development, I avoided mirrors. I had good height, posture, karate muscles—except where was my facial hair? Some of the guys in my class, think Zonko, already resembled primates. Cool! Me? I was sort of a pretty boy with smooth skin and those green eyes. If I admired any part of my body, it was the couple of scars on my ribs, leftovers from the balcony incident.

My four school friends and I were of like mind. We wore drooping jeans and oversized, limp tee shirts. We let our hair seek its own level, maybe in front of one eye or pooled on our shoulders. I alternated between a pony tail tamed by a rubber band, and bangs resembling a Lone Ranger mask, no comb involved. If anyone looked our way, we frowned disapproval like freaks on an album cover. This accomplished two things, cutting remarks from disgusted parents, and a blending-in during forbidden excursions.

Curfews? Nah, we were cagey. Our late-night discoveries in seamy areas included a fast and furious street race fleeing from cops short of the finish line; a low-rent topless bar that didn't ask for IDs as long as we carried plenty of cash, and the enticement to sit in for a rock band's jailed drummer in a wee-hours jam. Zonko knew somebody with an invitation to a garage, so we dropped by. Our instructions were to skip the massive sliding door, which would be locked; rather, we could walk in through a side entrance.

Guitar riffs and low voices told us it was the right place. Single file, we trailed into the heavy mist of pot. One overhead bulb allowed dim light through a shade of dust and dead bugs. The three players barely noticed us until I made myself right at home on the jailbird's sweet double base kit.

One guy looked vaguely familiar and I must have struck him the same way. We kept glancing at each other until he spoke.

"Carlos Montero, right?"

"Yeah?"

"You don't remember me, do you, drummer boy?"

"Not really."

He looked to be in his late thirties, with a week's beard and ratty hair. A patch of scalp showed through. He drew on a cigarette.

"Well, I remember you and I remember your old man, too, testifying against me when he didn't know shit. He might be interested to know I'm out."

"Out of what?"

He gave me a hard look.

"I guess you wouldn't care that he stole five years of my life. Did he tell you about that?"

"Nah," I said. "He only tells me important stuff."

Sneaking out to danger

Without taking his eyes off me, he bolted up and smashed his foot into the bass drum, sending it crashing.

"Whoa, man!" I stretched up an open hand. "Sorry, sorry," I said, stunned by his outburst.

We stood motionless. His face contorted with rage.

Finally he threw his head back, closed his eyes, and slowly exhaled a mighty breath. He hooked his foot on his chair leg, pulled it under him and reached for his guitar. As if nothing had happened, he shot a peace sign to my guys who were standing around with their mouths open. Cautiously, I rescued the drum.

He hunched over his guitar and strummed a few chords. His shoulders relaxed. He played a few measures before mouthing words that rattled my memory.

"Me and you...me and you, looking for greenness bending around a corner, oh yeah."

Holy crap, it was a meager-haired Angkor What!

He saw I recognized him and through a brown-toothed smile enlightened me.

"They picked me up for messing with you. You know damn well that wasn't the case. I've never touched little kids. I was just giving you a music lesson. So you know what?"

I waited.

"You and your daddy owe me one. That's what." Still smiling, he set his guitar aside, reached over to slip his hand around my arm. His grip tightened.

I pulled back, but he held fast and with his other hand, he patted my face.

"We'll play a little calypso number and you tap-tap on those skins and then we'll play something else, something real nice, okay?"

He didn't mean music. I jerked away and looked for support from his companions, a keyboardist and second guitar player. They were smirking. What the hell, I was in a den of pedophiles. What about my three buddies? Terrified, they had backed into a wall. No help there. Angkor turned their way.

"Hey, you rodents, get outside. I want to tell him a few things about his daddy."

He turned back to me and spoke close to my face.

"When your old man had me doing time, I got curious about him and I had a few years to look into it. Yeah, Emilio Montero, little movie actor, big scandal. The papers had a ball with that. You know all about it, don't you, baby?"

My friends seemed paralyzed. For once, Zonko's eyes were more conspicuous than his beard.

Angkor let go of me to jab a finger in their direction.

"Out! Now!" he shouted.

They stumbled away. Angkor rushed behind them, locked the side door and pocketed the key. The musicians took his action as a cue to leave. They glided through a door to the interior of the house. I heard a distant door slam.

Next thing I knew, Angkor bounded back and slid his arm around my shoulder.

I can persuade you, baby," he said. I felt his hand move down my side and cup into a caress.

A mass of disgust enveloped me. Years of Humberto's self-defense tactics kicked in. Muscle memory shot my right arm up into his diaphragm. My left hand chopped into his windpipe. He reeled backward, flying into the drum set. Pressing his neck and gasping for breath, he followed the snare and symbols as they careened to the hard floor. I sprinted for the door. It wouldn't budge. Dawn! Angkor had pocketed the key. I gave it my best kick, but no joy. Behind me, I heard drums clatter as Angkor regained his footing with alarming resilience.

Sneaking out to danger

He charged across the room. I pounded the door to get the attention of my friends outside. That mistake left me vulnerable.

A second later, Angkor grabbed my ponytail. He snapped my head back. In one motion, he swiveled me around with enough force to upset my balance. I smashed down against a workbench. The left side of my face crushed into wood and something heavy thudded against my neck. The reflection of the overhead light glinted into my struggling eyesight and I realized the flash came from a knife blade.

"Now it's my turn, little fucker. I'm going to show you some fun I learned in the joint. The guys teach you real good there."

I groped for his shoulders and bent my knees up to throw him off. My action only helped him pull at my pants.

"You're gonna like it, you're gonna like it," Angkor said in a frenzy.

"Dammit!" I yelled. "Get the fuck off me!"

That earned me a smack to the jaw with the knife handle protruding from his fist. The blow flattened me to the floor. I felt blood rushing down my cheek. My attention widened. I focused on, of all things, the dead insects in the ceiling fixture.

"Yeah," said Angkor. "Now the way we do this is you roll over like a good boy."

His fingers curled around my loosened waistband. I reacted with a surge of energy that sent him reeling backward. His watery eyes went into life-saving mode. True to his word, he had learned some sharp moves. We took turns yelling and pinning each other down. He was stronger than he looked, but I was younger. At one point, I flipped him into a chair. It tilted backwards, dumping him to the floor. He sprang up like an overgrown cat and shoved his head into my ribs. I went down with him sprawled on top of me. His moldy breath bathed my face.

"Take it easy, babykins," he said through a damaged smile. "We fight a little, we love a little, that's the way."

He was ripe for my much-practiced elbow and palm strikes. Sometimes you know, you really know, what you can do. With one lightning chop, I rearranged his jaw. From there out, I could have maimed him. To this day I believe that. No chance. Instead, a mighty thump and a crash wiped out all of Angkor What's obnoxious intentions.

One second Angkor was there. The next, he vanished.

I strained my painful neck upward to witness a slaughter.

Angkor's knife sailed near me to hit the floor. He was being pounded against the wall, flipped to the cement, kicked in the face, smashed in the chest, jerked upright and punched in the kidneys.

His attacker showed no mercy at the sound of ribs cracking, paid no heed to Angkor's blood, grunts and desperate cries. Finally, with a wimpy sound, Angkor crumpled to the floor.

Humberto grabbed up the knife and looked like he wanted to slice flesh.

"Oh, Jesus!" I yelled. "Don't do it, Humberto. He got the idea."

Without taking his eyes off Angkor's fetal position, Humberto threw the knife aside and reached out to help me to my feet. He took my bloody face in both hands for a brief inspection, and with trembling arms hugged me close in a show of relief and caring that I'll never forget. I had been taking his loyalty to the family for granted all those years. Now my pain wasn't all physical.

"Let's get out of here," he said.

I let Humberto guide me out across the door splinters. A fresh breeze slapped at my throbbing cheek, yet pain wasn't premier. Where were my friends? And the car we came in? Humberto noticed my anxiety.

"I told 'em to get their sorry butts home," he said. "The pervert's lovers took off, too."

Sneaking out to danger

We crossed the street toward his parked car.

"Get in," he said, hanging back to make a phone call. The way he lowered his voice gave me the impression he had contacted a police buddy to handle the mayhem we left behind.

When he slid into the driver's seat, Humberto handed me a grungy rag.

"Mop yourself up. I don't want you to spoil my dainty upholstery." His joke—both the rag and upholstery looked like accessories from a stable.

Soon he pulled into to an all-nighter and asked for a couple of icy drinks. He found a parking spot, dampened a wad of napkins, and handed the makeshift poultice to me.

As I dabbed at my oozing injuries, I asked him how he knew where to find me. How was it that he appeared at the height of peril? I once heard Pops explain that in ancient drama, such an improbability is called *deus ex machina,* an act of God to rescue a hopeless situation. Humberto's answer dumbfounded me as much as if stage machinery had lowered him into the garage.

"Little dumbass," he said, "I follow you every time you sneak out."

"No way, not every time."

"Every time. Does the name Titty-Titty Boom-Boom sparkle in your memory?"

"Aw, shit," I said through a tight smile. "Did you see her?"

"A generous amount."

Our salacious recollections of a shady club lowered us to equal ground until Humberto switched back to the firmness of the cop he once was.

"Your old man doesn't want to deny you some street smarts, but he expects you to survive the lessons. Now about tonight. Let's get our stories straight."

While contriving our move, he rubbed the reddened knuckles of his brawny hands. "How about we tell him you got into a little scuffle with some arrogant shit at a club and I saved you. You'll catch hell, but he won't have to agonize about the stinking hophead again."

"That first time—Angkor never touched me. He got put away for dealing drugs."

"I know. The slammer is where he got initiated into the down-under world."

"I could've saved myself."

"Think so?"

"Absolutely. It didn't start out right, but I was remembering the stuff you taught me."

"Glad to hear it. We'll still need to explain why you're so messed-up, right? Sneaking back into your room won't do it. In the morning, your folks might want to know why you're looking at your pancakes with only one squinty eye."

"I guess. What about you? What if Angkor goes to the police?"

Humberto laughed and shook his head at my innocence.

"And he tells 'em what? Like, Gentlemen, I was about to rape me a 16-year-old boy when this madman smashed down the door and nearly beat me to death?"

"What if he tries revenge?"

"Don't worry about that. I have plans for him if he survives tonight. Either way, you won't be hearing from him again. For starters, I think I made him bite his tongue in half."

8

Change of plans

My dark adventures ended abruptly that violent night. Humberto delivered me through the front door and abandoned me to my fate.

Mama, in her robe, glared, then jabbed her finger toward her head.

"You see these gray hairs? *Me estas volviendo loca!*" (You are driving me crazy!)

Pops lit into me, his dark eyes accusing, his voice level and cutting.

"What the hell do you think you were doing? Look at you—you're a disgrace. If it's your goal to put us in early graves, call the mortuary now. I'll look up the number."

"Sorry."

"Sorry won't do it!"

Mama winced at his tone.

"Okay, so what do you want?"

"Hey! Don't smart mouth me! Now you listen. And listen good."

A fresh billow of pain hit my temples. Pops' demands, way beyond a mere apology, and my guarded response amounted to a heated agreement.

In those few agonizing minutes, every detail of my plan to go to Stanford in Alex's tracks blew up. My parents said no, I'd be living at home and commuting to USC instead. They wanted to keep their eyes on me at home for four more years.

When the lecture ended, Mama fed me aspirin and gave me ice and a cloth to treat my bruises. I slunk up to my room and, wide awake, eased into bed with an almost impossible choice: Either relive the Angkor abuse in all its potential violence and humiliation, or force myself to concentrate on revising college plans. I strained to pretend Angkor never happened.

In comparing universities, I had checked out USC's journalism program a few months ago, and it definitely had appeal. It offered an early start on the latest media technology. I'd learn to tell stories digitally, using audio, video, tablets and standard photography. I could be a one-man journalistic band. I'd also give a nod to nature study because it played so well into camera work.

Besides the stay-home part, the flipside of my new plan was telling Pops I'd probably start up as a news reporter, in his words a maggot. He never explained that attitude. Now it reminded me of other things in my life that didn't add up.

Ricardo was brotherly to Alex. Why did he still pick on me? Did he know something I didn't? Was he right in saying I was found in a dumpster? Was I still unwanted?

Ricardo was nearly 10 years old when I joined the family. He would know if Mama had been pregnant. And he would resent being outside of their confidence, a circumstance I understood. That thought bore a mild surprise, a softening of attitude. It inspired a mind game: if my entire family were in mortal danger, say an earthquake or house fire, would I defend them with my life, and in what order? First Mama and the girls. No, first Alex, who would then help me save the girls and Mama and Pops. Assuming no choice, I'd save Ricardo. He was my brother, after all. But he'd be last. And as soon

Change of plans

as I got him out of danger, I'd follow my first instinct and punch him in the nose.

Another puzzle: the persistent kidnapping theme. Wasn't something fishy about the way my parents responded to the earlier Angkor incident? They lectured, yet didn't blame me. Instead, they warned of a more sinister possibility. No specifics, as usual—more of an exercise to ignite a little kid's vigilance.

Mama's reaction when she picked me up from day camp kick-started my curiosity. Did she know the woman who showed up briefly, the one who called me by name? Mama said no, but I never forgot how her voice choked to a whisper. I remembered Pop's expression, too.

Could the unnamed woman be my real mother?

Did she toss me in a dumpster? If she didn't care then, why should she care now?

My imagination accelerated. Could she be plotting a ransom note to Pops?

I remembered she had taken my picture, a fact I withheld from my parents.

What about the scandal remark? Chances were, Angkor was just a windbag. Someday maybe I'd look deeper into Pops' background. His voluminous scrapbook sat available in our library. I had read enough to notice the sparse mention of him as a movie actor. He had been a bit player, after all. Publicity picked up regarding his real estate successes and philanthropy. All the clips were favorable. That meant either Angkor was a vessel of bullshit or Pops had a highly selective pair of scissors.

9

Hurry, it's time to—what?

Nowhere in USC's syllabus does it mention disillusionment, how new imperatives can either scrap a long-held goal or dim its appeal. That's what happened to my Trojan drumline ambition when I turned 18. I learned that the summer camp and practice sessions would eat way too much study time.

My new daydream was to accumulate so many facts that I'd be eligible for Jeopardy. So my personal drums got relegated to now-and-then jams with here-and-there players—most of my wannabe musician friends drifted off to different institutions or enrolled in static indolence. None of us was Julliard material anyway. As for piano, my fingers exercised twice a month when Pops had his barbershop cronies over. Before retiring to the library for poker and brandy, they'd warble a few antediluvians in the music room. Pops insisted on my participation beforehand. In front of his friends, he made it sound like I couldn't wait to volunteer. A bit of show biz there, I decided, and pretended to roll with their nostalgia.

The poker game had been going on sporadically for years. Pops and Zack Foster, old friends from studio days, had a special bond, their insults and banter notwithstanding. Zack was the youngest of the group, a clever, charming, manipulative Hollywood type, a former studio publicist who now ran his own talent business and seemed to know everybody on either side of print. His specialty was guiding clients into camera range. He liked to say:

"My job is to put the shim in sham, to give a good name to artificiality."

One evening during my final year at USC he showed up with take-outs of one of Pops old Westerns.

"Stick around," he said to me, stroking his trim gray mustache. "You'll see me in a bit part as an Indian fighter—brilliant acting."

Pops, the ex-Indian, countered:

"He lasted exactly one scene. I dropped him with an arrow right off and saved the industry."

During a song fest the two sometimes drifted from the piano and talked in a corner as if they were carrying on a life parallel to everyone else's.

Then, so was I. With its feast of communication styles, J-School had become my obsession. I achieved a journalism student's ultimate experience, two internships, one at a television station and another at a small newspaper (credit Zack Foster's influence here). In addition to "convergent journalism," meaning group effort, I shot action, studio stills, videos, did voice-overs, downloaded relevant apps to my phone, covered campus events, wrote stories about city council meetings, sports and (my least favorite) celebrities. I topped all that with social media, tweeting and blogging, where useful.

I developed a cool bring-it-on demeanor. That was on the outside, as befitting my idea that a news photographer-writer should be fair, unemotional, and at all times a perfectionist while dragging around a burden of equipment, keeping batteries charged, and getting little sleep. On the inside, my nerves pinged around like a kennel of fleas.

After four intense years, I was graduated. I was also thinner

Hurry, it's time to—what?

and aimless. For the next few weeks, separating from my pillow was a ceremony of mid-afternoon.

One of those afternoons, I skipped a decent shower and still in thin pajama bottoms, thumped down the stairs for a lazy dive into the pool. I splashed up just as Mama and some of her twee lady friends, mimosas in hand, emerged from the house to gaze at her fragrant *Rosa* 'Double Delight' roses. I had no towel. My pajamas stuck to me, leaving nothing for the imagination. Mama's pampered skin tone turned the ruby shade of her garden blossoms. I played it cool by nodding to the ladies, and sauntering toward the door as if veiled nudity were a Montero signature.

The episode put my lassitude in sharp focus. Mama dropped bomb-hints about the positive merits of employment. She reminisced about her one long-ago job, how it gave her important insights to the working world. Finally, turning to Pops, she made her point.

"If the newspapers aren't hiring, Carlos could help Carmela at your office. She loves it. Give him a start there too, okay?"

Pops raised an eyebrow—not an answer, a signal. Soon they went to their bedroom and closed the door.

That Friday evening when the quartet materialized in the music room, I was at the grand, left-handing an oldie, a soft bumble boogie bass. Zack, drink in hand, leaned against the piano in total appreciation. His shoulders bounced to dance floor memories. "Yeah, you tell 'em, man," he said. "That's the real stuff."

"You're not that old, Zack," I said.

"Hell, I can't even remember when I was your age."

He tilted his glass for the final drops. They turned into a shower of ice cubes against his mustache and down his shirt. I improvised the octave trill and ominous bass of silent movie villains.

"Knock it off. Jeez." Zack's groan was half disgust with himself, half amused. He dabbed the spill with a paper napkin.

"Listen," he said, "your father claims you were big stuff in journalism school. But you haven't set your course yet, right? Why don't you let me pull a few strings?"

"Have something in mind?"

"I know a newspaper editor in Houston, good friend of mine, who's looking for talent. Of course, you have to prove yourself with a good résumé and interview."

Leave town? Nah, I thought, Pops would never sanction a move like that.

"I hear you're an excellent cameraman. That's a major plus today. This editor—he's a nice guy. We've traded favors in the past. You could say I'm his Southern California recruiter."

"I don't know anything about Houston."

"Who does?" Zack shrugged. "When they're not having hurricanes, they have astronauts. Maybe you could get yourself embedded on a shuttle to Mars." He turned to the bantering threesome seated behind him. "Emilio! Wouldn't that give you some bragging rights?"

"What?"

"What I just said."

"What did you just say?"

Zack turned back to me. "Have you noticed? You can't have an intelligent conversation with these drunks. Play something bittersweet, Carlos. How about "I Wanna Go Home Again, Arlene?" My mother used to sing it while she was ironing."

"Don't know that one. How about "I'll Take You Home Again, Kathleen?" "

"Sure, smartass, that's it. Play it, son. I could use a good cry—lost two hundred clams the last time to that avaricious guy over there," he said, pointing at Pops. "Carlos, you should be ashamed to be his son. He's a thief."

Hurry, it's time to—what?

Pops laughed. "What are you talking about, fool? You're the luckiest poker player in the state—your wife still works!"

* * *

In less than a week, I got a surprise call.

The man identified himself as William Garon, editor of the *Houston Herald*.

"I understand you might be right for a position here," he said, sounding relaxed and friendly.

Zack's memory had outfoxed his booze.

Garon asked to see my résumé, my best photography and, he hoped, some video and writing samples.

"It's about time we make progress here. We need to grab more of the multimedia audience. We should be appealing to younger readers, if that isn't an oxymoron," he said. "I'll be frank with you—our circulation is down. That's a common story with newspapers now. We're thinking of kicking up our on-line *Herald*."

He admitted that *The Herald*'s content didn't stand up well in a recent poll.

"So we have some fresh assignments in mind for the right talent."

He described a recent stir in his area, an unusual archeological find.

"I want it covered from beginning to end. Breaking news, of course, but something more lasting for the schools. It's a good opportunity to offer new reporting styles, the stuff they're teaching in J-school these days."

We carried on a bit, with Garon recalling a frugal period spent as a reporter at the *Riverside Press Enterprise* and touring the historic Mission Inn. I offered that I'd never been to Texas.

"No? Well, you'll find a few palm trees here and some interest in fine arts, lots of restaurants, just like Los Angeles. But we aren't as laid back, we aren't as routinely quirky as LA. No mountains. No earthquakes, either."

Sounds dull, I thought, but I warmed to the attention, and told him he could find the heart and soul of my work on my blog.

"Perfect," he said. "I'll phone you our decision."

10

Nightmare in the archives

Throughout the next week, I did a good job of not thinking about moving to Texas, which I suspected might be a backward jungle of hayseed and horse manure. As a diversion, I dated different girls for lunch, dinner, movies and Disneyland. That should have been enough to dispel apprehension. Not so. Finally, I hit on an activity that might work. I'd do that long-delayed research of Pops' movie years.

My reluctance is hard to explain. I guess I didn't want to rattle my sense of family stability, the string of ideas and experiences that comfort by their familiarity. Looking back, though, I realize I had buried disturbing details deep in my subconscious.

Information was available. I only had to ask. An apologetic librarian pointed to the basement where a cache of older newspaper and magazine archives not yet scanned sat stacked in heavy binders.

I turned dusty entertainment sections to the years Pops donned war paint for a living and learned that gossip columns rarely mentioned him until he was offered a big break as a leading man in a retro Latin musical. He'd been chosen because he was sophisticated looking, dashing and, yes, splendidly Hispanic. His leading lady would be a young hottie named Estella. Fascinated Hollywood reporters gushed about the couple's magnetism despite a significant age difference, and about their South American dance numbers in rehearsal. One ventured to declare them the reborn Fred and Ginger. Not once did I see mention of Pops' private life. By lingering Hollywood rules, it might have dampened his appeal to learn he had a wife and four kids.

All this was new to me. I kept turning pages, thinking how interesting it was to see Pops schmoozing with this babe in sexy dance costumes. I wondered what Mama thought—she'd be home with the four and me on the way.

Then I turned another page and all hell broke loose.

A headline screamed that Estella was missing. Her photo, credited to the studio clips, took up a quarter of the front page. She wore so much dark hair, likely a wig, and so much make-up that it looked like an ad for an ethnic cosmetics firm.

Follow-up stories described how Hollywood went berserk, first suspecting an offensive publicity stunt to promote the musical. But more evidence indicated she'd been abducted. Initial sympathetic gossip turned speculative, then brutal. Finally I came to a jarring account. My pulse hammered as I read and reread the day's lead story. Emilio Montero was in jail, it said. Police had arrested him on suspicion of murder.

11

Escape in a daze

Articles written a year after Estella's disappearance took a broader view. One writer compared the public furor with another sensational scandal, the Black Dahlia mutilation of the 1940s. During that infamous panic, a horde of police from LA and other cities got involved, and a ludicrous number of people were suspect, including an investigating officer. In the Estella case, the same way it happened many decades ago, anyone who had the slightest acquaintance with the "victim" was a person of interest, and that included Pops, the man who held her close in dance rehearsals.

I read with relief that he was released from jail for lack of evidence. Without a body, a confession or a witness, a murder charge might be premature. Along with dozens of others, he remained under watch, even as several crazies confessed in order to attain notoriety.

It wasn't just the dancing role that ignited rumors about Pops and Estella. They had been having coffee together in the commissary; they were seen chatting after work; her scarf turned up in his dressing room. Gossip columnists chewed away at every crumb. Photographers dogged him. One photo showed Pops at our front door, surrounded by news photographers. A shadowy figure in the music room window had to be Mama. I wondered if our tall, stone wall was a byproduct of the invasion.

I walked away from my research marveling at the damage gossip can do. USC's School of Journalism mission statement came to mind:

Every human advancement or reversal can be understood through communication.

But what if the communication is flawed? Finally, I understood Pops' revulsion toward gossip reporters, in his word, 'scumbags.'

The Rio-themed movie starring Estella and Pops foundered under the weight of it all. Pops' contract was rescinded. He could afford to shrug films off because he'd already experienced real estate bonanzas which he celebrated by buying a grand Spanish-style house.

My research left me dazed. Estella was never found. If she had been murdered, the perpetrator could still be at large. For several nights I lay awake gripped by my runaway imagination and all manner of "what if's." The worst, based on my parents' habitual secrecy, kept me stirred up. What if the murderer lay asleep in the downstairs bedroom, next to my trusting mother? What if one of his barbershop gigs was actually a lie, an excuse to bury the body in the Mojave Desert? My timing was off there—the quartet hadn't materialized yet, but my macabre fantasies danced with the idea.

Those wretched thoughts sidetracked me. I started getting mechanical stares and vague reactions to spoken words, such as, "Did you hear what I said?" and "Where is your mind?" I didn't remember much about a telephone invitation from William Garon, the Houston editor, or my packing for the flight, or even my parents' storm of cautions and instructions.

Not until I was halfway there, already over El Paso, did I feel a sense of separation and the irony of it. My dread of moving from LA suddenly flipped into anticipation for the independence and a new life away from questions without answers.

12

Writer vs. photographer

Reality kicked in when I stood before the receptionist on the third floor of the *Houston Herald*. She twisted the top on a bottle of polish and blew on her nails before ushering me into the glass-walled office of the managing editor.

Garon, sleeves rolled up, elbows on his desk, talked into a phone. He signaled recognition and cut his conversation short. With a hand stretched over a pile of proofs and a jumbled in-box, he welcomed me.

"Glad to have you on board, Carlos."

He was an oak of a man with a big forehead, thinning hair and thick glasses. From our genial phone conversation, I had pictured a milder-looking guy.

"I'm already hired?"

"We're impressed with your work. You're young and trained to roll with the changes ahead. We hope you like us."

The power of approval! I asked him exactly what the paper expected of me.

"Have a seat. Let's talk about it," he said.

Garon explained how they had been late in embracing the internet by denying that newsroom culture had changed all around the country. Hold-outs are gamblers—that's clear now, even for the broadcast field, he said. He blamed the economy and the advertising slump. In a recent survey, he said, *The Herald*'s internet efforts were declared a journalistic disaster.

"We're trying to persuade some of our aging wordsmiths to carry a video camera and laptop and get acquainted with social media. You can't imagine the resistance. One of our reporters threatened to chain himself to the water fountain. We calmed him down with a week off. It takes a fresh mind to make all the sudden turns. The photo chief is struggling big-time—that's Rob Blaisdale. He'll give you both general and specific assignments.

"Meantime, keep up with your blog. It's interesting. We're anxious to see your take on local material."

He leaned back in his chair, clasped his hands over his chest, and angled his chin in a thoughtful pose to summarize the paper's predicament.

"Our publisher needs to realign his thinking away from the idea that newspapers are a one-a-day miracle. He's slow in catching on that we need to be a 24/7 operation, with streaming news on the internet. We need..."

Garon interrupted himself, looked past me toward the receptionist and snatched up the phone.

"Susan, was that Holly Bryant who just walked by? Send her in."

A young woman sailed through the door.

I saw a windblown mass of wavy light brown hair surrounding a "what's up?" expression. She was dressed in an oversized denim shirt and loose jeans, its legs pooled over sneakers. I felt the electricity of her blue-gray eyes scanning me head-to-toe.

I stood for the introduction. Garon did not.

Writer vs. photographer

"Holly, meet Carlos Montero. This is Holly Bryant, our capable science writer."

Her name was familiar because I'd read a few issues of *The Herald* before coming here. I noticed her byline because she had produced a skillful account of the recent space shot at Cape Canaveral. Bryant was much younger than I imagined, probably my age.

"I've been hearing about you," she said.

I smiled at her while Garon streamed on.

"I want you to show Carlos around, help him get acquainted. He can use Charlie Patterson's desk in Features, but he'll also answer to Photo, so take him around there to meet folks. Now, Holly, you'll have to give Carlos background on the archeological assignment. I want you guys to team up and cover it from all angles."

He glanced at his watch. "Take him to lunch on your expense account."

"Love to! May we use your club membership?"

"Nice try. Not the way you're dressed."

"Neat, huh?"

She pulled at her pant legs as if to take a bow. "I scouted the dig area early this morning—these are my androgynous dig duds."

Looking slightly amused, Garon got back to business.

"Keep in mind, folks, we need to coordinate developing news and do a special section later, heavy on pictures for print and some video for online. Think of it as a documentary," he said to me. "Something the schools can use. I'd like to see some of our work published as e-books. We're committed to education in this district."

Holly nodded. "I've already outlined the whole project."

"Good. Give Carlos a copy."

"It's still in my head."

"I thought..."

"Won't take me long." She turned to me. "I'll sketch it out for you at lunch, okay? I even know what kind of photos it needs."

Attractive though she might be, I distrusted her immediately. Reporters have a bad habit of specifying shots and saying "my photographer" as if they are holding a leash.

"So, you're a photographer?" I asked.

Garon answered for her.

"Oh, yes, indeed. We gave her a small starter camera. She came back with a picture of the inside of her handbag."

She assumed a fake hangdog look.

"Okay, so I haven't mastered it yet."

"That means you didn't bother to read the directions. It's a common defect around here, ignoring the inevitable."

"It's true, it's true," she agreed. "Especially the old-timers. But I'm optimistic. We'll all come around."

"I'll need that in writing," said Garon through a lop-sided grin. "Carlos, please give her some basics—like show her how to aim a camera where it counts. Now, you two go on and enjoy your lunch. When you get back, Carlos, check in with personnel."

He dismissed us to answer his ringing telephone. I realized I had barely spoken, but at least I did a lot of nodding.

We didn't have a lot to say to each other as Holly guided me through the downtown tunnel system's noontime crowd, which had me walking variously beside and behind her. I noticed her good height and healthy stride. We elbowed past several retail shops, quick-serves and lower lobbies of major buildings. Finally we entered a small, frigid restaurant. Not until we were seated, facing each other in a booth, did she start a conversation, and she surprised me with her sensitivity to my earlier remark.

"I didn't mean to imply back there that I'll tell you what or how to shoot. It's just that I tend to see the whole product in my head before I begin. Some people do outlines. I do mental imaging. It's helpful—subject to revision by circumstance, of course."

Writer vs. photographer

"Fair enough. Let's hope my interpretations meet your high standards."

She swept her hair back on one side and tilted her chin. "You're a typical photographer."

"That's insulting. How can you tell so soon?"

"You're protective of your craft. The guys I've worked with are congenial but they rarely tolerate suggestions."

"There's a reason. Suppose you write a story and someone says you missed the whole point and tells you what to do instead. That makes you subservient."

She laughed. "I believe you just described my first six weeks at *The Herald*."

She asked me polite questions about my background until our food arrived. The waiter shifted table junk toward the wall and wedged plates between us. Holly interspersed eating with a scanty explanation of the archeological assignment.

"We can talk some more about it on the way down next week. For print, I've lined up the professor in charge. He's interesting when he goes one-on-one with his students and, I hesitate to mention this, you might like that for video. If they turn up something unexpected, we can shoot for breaking news."

"How'd you train for your job?"

"I have a degree in journalism from the University of Texas. I graduated earlier than most because I skipped two grades along the way—brilliant me, model daughter of a teacher—so I've been working for a couple of years. I was writing general features when they needed someone to cover a space shot because the regular guy was…"

She recanted. "Actually, they waited a whole month before giving me the science writer title."

"I read a post on your blog before I came here."

"Which one?"

"About synthesizing life forms."

"Yes, how scientists are working on piecing together protein modules. Someday they'll create tissue in the lab, a decent steak even, no cow required."

We seemed to be on the same track.

"How do you feel about insects?" I asked.

"That's an odd question. It depends."

"On what?"

"On whether they're out in the woods or in my house."

My interest picked up. "What kind would be in your house?"

"In this climate? Anything, but mainly big cockroaches— the kind that fly at your face."

"Yeah? Would you catch one for me? I'll do a macro shot of it."

"Are you insane? Those nasty bugs are filthy. Just thinking about them crawling on my dishes—and to smack one makes all their insides squish out on the carpet while they're still wiggling and then you have to scoop it up. Oh, please!"

I drummed a fork against the table, the Trojan Fight Song, and stared at her. She had just cast an unforgivable barb at my lifelong pursuit of entomologic photography. What could be so insane about capturing a *Periplaneta americana*?

I decided to be reasonable.

"Roaches aren't as filthy as people think," I said. "They don't bite. Well, they might bite a sleeping baby, but they'd rather hide from you."

She learned toward me. With her voice good-natured, but strained through self-righteous amusement, she summed me up.

"You are a smart ass."

Before I could retort, she continued, "We'll make a formidable team—me treating my photographer as a slave, and you carrying on as a royal prince of your domain."

"Well put, but I'm enlightened. I no longer require deep bowing.

Writer vs. photographer

A small curtsy will do."

"Thanks. That's noble."

Her smile fading, she shifted attention to a slice of carrot on her plate, pushing it one way, then another with her fork. Finally she let go.

"I know something you don't know."

"Try me."

"Heavy rumors are flying around the paper. One is that it's about to be sold to a media conglomerate. Another is that you were hired at a ridiculous salary for your recent training and experience in technology. *The Herald* is desperate to adopt more relevant tech procedures solely for buyer-appeal. Maybe you noticed the scaffolding outside. A facelift, even."

"Any more?"

"Lots. If the paper changes hands and direction, most of the old-timers and even some savvy newcomers will be sacked. When I first arrived, everyone was so happy and friendly, I wanted to slap them, bring them to their senses. Now everyone is suspicious and on edge. What I'm saying is—and for some reason I'm being protective here—don't expect to be Mr. Popularity, no matter how digital you are."

13

A dead man's desk

Holly's talk on the way back to the office touched on routines I might expect, including my urgent need to get assigned a company van. Back on the editorial floor, we entered a U-shaped cubicle farm where she introduced me to co-workers—the anorexic food editor slouched behind stacks of releases and new cookbooks, the mini-skirted design editor, the travel writer wincing into his telephone, saying, "Hawaii? Yes ma'am, it's friendly to Americans. What have you heard?"

Holly pointed to a desk.

"That's yours, Carlos." Light dust traced the outline of a removed machine.

She made a phone call.

"Dennis? We have a new person down here at Charlie's desk. He needs computer stuff."

I asked, "What happened to what's-his-name—Charlie—the guy who sat here? Get a better job?"

"He died."

"Oh."

"Yes, several months ago."

She lowered her voice. "He overdosed. Charlie was a really nice guy, good science writer, but he got the flu and mixed alcohol with his medication. Big-time. A bunch of us went to his funeral. He was only 28."

"Tough."

"True. His desk has been empty ever since because *The Herald* got stingy about hiring—that's why they took a chance on me to fill his job. The paper was beginning to look silly using wire copy when top research facilities are right here in town."

She pointed at a nearby cluttered cubicle. Its angle put it in easy view from my station.

"That's my desk," she said. "We had a fire department inspection last week and they condemned it. I just haven't had time to go through my stuff." She remembered: "Oh, I'm supposed to take you to Photo. Follow me."

To make conversation, I asked how long it might take to memorize all the peculiar hallways, turns and step-downs in this old building. Holly explained that it was a cut-and-paste job of three structures. In yesteryear, they stood for independent purposes and because their floors had no reason to match each other, conjoining required short flights of steps here and there.

"Just watch your step," she said, and I wondered how meaningful that phrase might become.

At the end of one hallway, we found secretary Teesha sitting inside the photography department's entrance. When she heard I was their new hire, she handed me a van request form.

"I'll need it back today with a copy of your driver's license," she said. Her firm expression indicated authority.

Next in line was Rob Blaisdale, short and pale, except for incongruous strawberry cheeks and faded red hair. After a handshake, he nodded and cast his eyes sideways in listening mode while Holly recited her latest dig needs. A couple of telephones tried to drown her out. With an abrupt turn to me, Blaisdale asked, "What kind of equipment do you have?

I named my current inventory which includes a sharp audio adapter, and was about to go into detail of gadgets when he interrupted.

"That should do it," he said. "You need to talk to Teesha about our routine and don't mess with her rules, she'll run you up a dirt road. You need any lenses? We have a 50-50 plan here. After two years they're yours."

I declined, knowing one more device could compromise my backbone. With that, Blaisdale offered a distracted handshake and chased after one of his department's urgencies. Because he didn't seem especially interested in me, I wondered if he had been involved in my hiring, if he had even seen my résumé and portfolio. Holly's assessment of staff mood indicated otherwise: the overlords were not sharing information or objectives. Since I was the new arrival—that thought left me feeling disengaged from both extremes.

Back in Features after checking in with Personnel, I took my place at the late Charlie Patterson's desk and explored its drawers. Except for a NASA identification pin bearing Patterson's name, and a few odds and ends in the pencil drawer, they were clean. I dumped the stuff into the wastebasket.

A ka-thunk ka-thunk announced arrival of the I.T. desk man dragging computer essentials on a dolly. He looked to be in his late twenties but could have been a model for a casket company. Moisture settled in his frown. He smelled like medicine.

The waste basket caught his attention.

"What'd you throw away?"

"Nothing special, some old pencils and junk."

"I'm Dennis. I'm here to set you up with our intergalactic technology," he said while snatching up the NASA tag. "I'm kind of sentimental about anything Patterson left behind," he explained. "We were roommates."

I rolled my chair out of the way while Dennis dusted the desk surface with a soft yellow cloth, flung a cord about like a lasso, lifted the slender monitor in place with a grunt, attached the keyboard, and punched buttons. He grabbed an extra office chair from halfway across the room, dropped onto it with a sigh, and trundled back to the machinery.

"All right, now, let's have lesson *numero uno*."

He cast a glassy stare at me and attempted a friendly look. I rolled back even more.

"No, come closer," he coaxed. "You have to watch the screen while I explain. The editorial system uses three windows at the same time. Your editor can access them, so save the porn for home use."

Thin fingers danced over the keyboard as he talked. Little windows flew in front of big windows. He paused to rattle his windpipe and dab his forehead with a tissue. If he could work like that while sick, I wondered how would he perform while healthy?

"Sorry," he said, "I'm just getting over the flu. Or not. And I'll tell you something, the attitudes around here are anything but therapeutic. All over the building, it's like they just sack somebody and then expect the survivors to take up the slack. I'm surprised they actually hired you, no offense."

He plugged in the final wire.

"Now listen up, I'm going to show you how to work this in proper sequence," he said. "It's so simple, but to be honest, editorial people have more trouble than anyone in the building." He whispered, "Especially the food editor. That woman can hit keys in combinations that cause a rolling outage all over the city."

With a single stroke, he made the windows vanish.

"I shut it down," he said. "Now I want you to start it up and do exactly what I did."

A dead man's desk

"Okay, sure. What did you do?"

His deep sigh ended with a cough spasm. I rolled my chair back. "Never mind, I'll work it out," I said.

"I expect you will," said Dennis. "You have that rare appearance of intelligence. Call me anytime. I am your compu-slave."

He stood for a final word.

"You may not see me again. I hear the executives are working nights on a new butchering plan." He patted the computer. "Well, good luck." With that, he rumbled away pushing his empty dolly.

Holly had been observing us.

"Poor Dennis," she said. "He used to be the Help Desk comedian—kept us all laughing. Now he's worried about his job and grieving at the same time."

Without further concern, she turned to her desk, slipped on earphones and shoved a stack of papers aside to make room for her latest story components.

14

A cozy offer

The mammoth discovery story broke ahead of my arrival in Houston, before I inherited a dead man's desk.

Could there be remnants of an extinct elephant (*genus Mammuthus*) on the flat Texas Gulf Coast? Experts, satisfied with such finds in cold, northern regions, never considered it possible for the animal to stray so far south. That's why it was such a big deal when a sand pit operator recognized an ancient bone in the scoop of his backhoe. According to one of the stories, he all but stumbled in his rush to get to the land phone inside his trailer office where he called the *Houston Herald* and asked to speak to the science writer. That was Holly Bryant. She asked him to e-mail a photo to a paleontologist she knew. After examining the photo, the expert sent Holly an unscientific one-word message: "Wow!"

On my first day at the job, I stayed late to re-create Dennis' magic finger act. The computer, resentful at first, finally let go of the archives I needed, a couple of stories quoting amazed paleontologists. I called them for follow-ups.

The next morning during our drive to the site, Holly shared more details.

By the time I entered the drama, a large grid occupied the

burial area. College kids in T-shirts and khaki shorts were all over the place with brushes and sifters. The pit owner, an enlightened sort of fellow, had shut down business in that portion of his property and even provided a lawn chair for the presiding professor.

With one of my two cameras equipped with a small recorder mounted on the hot shoe, I gathered students' impressions of the dig. They got into my idea of assuming their audience was little kids already cozy with prehistoric creatures, thanks to kiddy TV. I decided the edited video might include a couple of animated dinosaur characters acting as hosts.

Next, I climbed up on an idle backhoe to pan the site with a telephoto lens. Nice video. Then, an opportunity. My zoom picked up a girl in a wide-brimmed hat casting a mean shadow everywhere except on her shy smile and loose V-neckline. When she leaned over to brush at her find—a forty-thousand year-old tooth—her T-shirt fell forward just enough to be interesting. Back down I went, this time for a pleasant chat while I captured the girl in both still and video shots.

Holly, equipped with iPhone to record and reporter's notebook for backup, hovered over Professor Terrance Loder from the state university. He was thin and weathered, his cheeks looking like twin pieces of toast. As I walked up for a profile shot, she was leaning into his rapt attention.

"The planet is a thriving life form," he said. "But I tend to give it more credit as a hungry burial ground. Anything that lives has only a miniscule contact. Not to be morbid, death is forever, which is handy for a paleontologist. You can find fossils all over the U.S. This beloved country is a massive cemetery."

Our stay ended when an invited study group from the University of Houston waved to Loder from the wire gate. He jumped up from his chair to greet them.

"We have to go," Holly said. "Thanks a million. Oh, one more

A cozy offer

thing. Could you furnish me with a copy of your field journal?"

His hesitation yielded to the lure of the spotlight.

"An unusual request, young lady, rarely granted. However, for you, yes, I'm certain I can arrange that."

I believe Holly could have asked him for his debit card or pin code, and he would have complied. At that moment I got insight to her reporting technique. By assuming intense interest in her subject's field, and by asking research-based questions, she granted old storytellers the satisfaction of sounding fresh and pertinent.

She also picked up on my technique. Walking toward the van, she turned it loose.

"I saw you hovering over that girl with the hat."

"And?"

"I wondered which mammalian discovery you had in mind."

"Good observation. I was gathering contextual data for dimensions."

"Interesting," she said. "And what was your estimate?"

"Size 34D, I think."

I expected her to appreciate my levity. Instead, she looked reproving.

We stashed our gear and an unintentional sprinkling of shoe sand in *The Herald* van and checked our phones for emails or texts from Photo and the news editor. During the first few miles toward the city, Holly leaned her head back and closed her eyes. She stirred only to reach for a bottle of water.

"Tired?"

I was fishing for her mood.

"No. I'm arranging the story in my mind. Better now than at the office."

At that point, she switched from plotting to input on her laptop.

That impressed me. I wondered if I shouldn't put my creativity to test while dodging insanity on the Gulf Freeway.

But fate had another idea. Just when the city skyline eased upward out of the horizon, I hit the brakes. Something screwy was going on between the freeway and feeder—a man chasing a goat that had bolted from a trailer. Abruptly, it was the goat chasing the man in a tight circle.

I grabbed my camera, flew out of the van, jumped the guard rail and ran down the incline. Brakes screeched behind the van and I had a fleeting worry about Holly's safety. But this was a natural. I got shot after shot of the action and managed to capture the decisive moment, when the goat charged from behind and lifted the guy off the ground to advance him about three feet. The victim rebounded, faced the animal and screamed obscenities in Spanish. Outrage had an effect. The goat gave him a haughty look. But yikes, he spotted me, another lowlife biped. He positioned his head for a new charge.

Raising my camera high, I did a contorted dance that inspired some rubber-necking guy in the background to yell, "Git him, Billy! Git him!" Inexplicably, the animal changed direction and returned to the trailer on his own placid terms. He even had the nerve to yawn.

Breathing hard and sweating, I heaved back up the incline to the van and found Holly wiping tears and laughing. I refused to comment, instead fiddled with the air conditioner until it blew a gale.

Once we got moving, she popped a question unrelated to the goat incident.

"Are you still staying in a hotel?"

"I am."

My stiff reply reflected frustration on that subject. Though convenient to the newspaper, my downtown quarters prolonged a feeling of dislocation. Over the weekend I even experienced a few pangs of homesickness that my calls to California didn't pacify. I added, "I'm more than ready to find an apartment. Any suggestions?"

A cozy offer

"One," she said. "Of course, I'm not sure of your requirements. Maybe you can afford one of those luxury high-rise condos. If so, this won't fill the bill. It's a modest roommate type of place, in an older part of town on a tree-lined street."

"Nah, I'm not excited about having a roommate."

"I know what you mean. But the bedrooms are on opposite sides, separated by a shared kitchen and living-dining area. There's really no need for a lot of communication. None, if you are a dine-out person."

"Well, maybe I can take a look. Is someone already living in the other half?"

"Yes," she said. "Me."

15

Some rough spots

My goat photo made page one with my dumb mistake. The three-column picture appeared without my credit line. Instead, the credit read: *Herald staff photo.*

In hopes of getting a correction in the next edition for the sake of the record, I mentioned the omission to the picture editor, a glum lump of a woman in her late thirties, hunched over a computer in the city room. Taking her time, she unglued herself to face me with a look that suggested she'd been waiting for my whine.

"It's only fair," she said. "You didn't bother getting an ID of the man in the picture, did you?"

True, I'd been in a god-awful hurry to save my butt. I decided not to elaborate. With more solicitous wording, I also asked why my clever caption wasn't used. It would have referred to the ballistic male goat as a nondairy creamer.

Her curt reply:

"Obtuse. It's doubtful readers would get the double-entendre. Excuse me, I'm on deadline."

She turned a cold back to me and resumed typing.

I'd been slammed in the butt after all. Or, had I encountered an ominous sample of workplace resentment and discontent?

Tangle of Secrets

My desk would seem a good haven, yet who should be sitting there but Dennis.

"Hi, Carlos," he said. He sounded and looked much healthier than he was on our initial meeting. "I wondered if..."

"If what?"

"Would you like to take a coffee break with me somewhere?"

"Can't, Dennis. Thanks, though."

"Okay." His shoulders drooped. "I used to come down here a lot when Patterson sat at this desk. He was a special friend. We could always talk to each other, from back in high school." He forced a smile. "Maybe some other time?"

"Yeah, sure, we'll see."

Evidently he noticed enough compassion in my face to reveal his worry.

"Everybody on our floor is expecting lay-offs. I wonder if you've heard anything."

"Not a thing, Dennis. You're asking the wrong guy. I'm too new here to be trusted with inside information."

"I don't know. Maybe. Okay, see you later."

He shuffled away and I reclaimed my chair.

I must have been staring into space again experiencing tension relief when I heard my name.

A hand waved in front of my eyes. It was a smiling Holly.

"Some of us are meeting at a joint called Coffee Grounds after work. Want to come?"

Hadn't I just declined a coffee invitation? But that was Dennis. This was Holly.

"Sure," I said.

Turned out it was a gripe session, which would have held Dennis spellbound, had he been invited. Four of us squeezed into a booth and two more scraped up chairs to launch complaints. Hicks, the travel writer, speculated that his job would end as soon as the paper was sold to a penny-pinching syndicate with a one-for-all travel section. He predicted it would be compiled by somebody's mentally challenged nephew up East.

Gilbert, a general assignments reporter, asked, "So, famous psychic, what will you do in that event?"

"I dunno, what do food stamps taste like?" Hicks asked. "Can you get 'em with gravy?"

Several absent editors got speared for their ceaseless dictates and unappreciative attitudes, or in the case of an elderly desk man, for his senile ways.

"His style book dates back to Gutenberg," said Paul, a metro reporter. "I used the expression 'willy-nilly' in a story and he changed it to William-nilly."

"No way," said Hicks. "You made that up."

Paul's non-committal shrug left room for speculation.

Sitting across from me, Holly looked big-eyed and perky with her hair gathered high in a silver clip. She nodded through all the grievances, and offered her own.

"It's the writing coach from UH who's driving me nuts," she said. "He dropped by today to gawk over my shoulder and make me delete a semi-colon. He despises them, says they weaken a story. He told me I may use a semi-colon only on my birthday and on Christmas."

Hicks laughed. "So, would that occur the same day—the reason your name is Holly?"

"You'd think. But Mom got my name from a romance novel. I was born on September 14. That, by the way, gives you guys just a few days to shop."

"Or not," said Hicks. "Would you settle for a packet of releases from the Outer Hebrides Tourism Industry Association?"

Holly looked pained. "If that's the best you can do, sure. How heavy is it?"

When I got back to my hotel room, it was still early enough in California to call Mama with the news.

"I'm moving in with the science editor."

"How fine of him to ask you," she said. "That's a load off my mind. I hope he lives in a nice neighborhood close to a police substation."

Her assumption saved me a lot of conversation. I gave her the new address and asked her to ship some stuff I had packed should the move turn permanent. The thing I most regretted leaving was my graduation gift, a sexy convertible. From day one, the emerald wonder machine and I molded to each other and I began to understand Pops' devotion to his relic Ford.

After hanging up, I corralled my belongings from the hotel bath and bedroom, and then hit the sack. The idea, I believed, was to fall asleep, but something (the perpetual pour of coffee?) was keeping me alert to every hotel noise. I reviewed the less-than-perfect day, the short time I'd been in Houston, the events that brought me here, the emotions I couldn't shake about Pops' background. I'm not much of a drinker, more of a health nut. But in this never-quite-dark room with its ghostly timeline of previous guests, with scrapes and scars on the furniture that can't be offset by freebee cosmetics, I saw why people slurped booze to brace up their vagabond nights.

My cell phone's ersatz marimba ring startled me. Let it not be Mama, I thought—I can't handle any more of her invented terrors.

Prayer answered. It was Holly.

"Hey, girl, what's up?"

"The maid came today, so your quarters are all spiffy. You have brand new bedding, even new towels and soap. When do you think you'll move in?"

On a lunch hour, I had inspected the place for livability and liked it—a lot. Same as her office cubicle, it was a bit Holly-cluttered, but she had a helper once a week to tidy up. My designated bedroom even had an alcove for a sizeable desk which would accommodate both a computer and macro photography. I promised myself not to mention insects.

"Any time," I said. "I'm already packed."

"So come on over."

"Now?"

"Why not? It's only midnight. I'll be up. I still have notes to type."

16

Togetherness, sort of

I paid two months' rent in advance and shared the cost of the maid. As Holly indicated earlier, she kept our living arrangement equal and quasi-separate. Occasionally we'd meet at the mailboxes or refrigerator. After she made a point of sharing a package of bakery treats, I reciprocated by stashing a quart of triple-chocolate ice cream in the freezer. Neither of us entertained visitors, so rules were just a matter of tactful standards.

Only one conduct required unreserved expression:

"If you want to read in the living room," she said, "you can sit in my favorite chair unless I'm already in it. That might be awkward."

Three weeks after I'd moved in, Holly approached me in the kitchen.

"I have a favor to ask," she said.

"Ask."

"My Mom is coming in from Austin Saturday. Would you mind letting her sleep in your room for one night?"

"The bed isn't big enough for both of us."

"Gross, Carlos, I mean would you mind staying in a hotel for one night? I'll pay."

For no specific reason, I felt grumpy and considered this an imposition.

"I suppose. Yeah, it'll give me an excuse to spend the weekend in LA with my sex-starved girlfriend."

"Thanks. Do that."

"You're welcome. I will." Already I wondered why I thought she'd care. Then she gave me a clue:

"She must be quite a tolerant woman."

"Meaning?"

"I mean, to put up with your finger drumming, your rat-a-tat rat-a-tat."

"That bothers you?"

"Not especially. But it's a distraction, rhythmic though you are."

She went spastic. "Like, rat-a-tat rat-a-tat boom boomity boomity boom!"

I pretended alarm, but had to smile. The girl was a comic.

With "Parrrump! Parrump!" she waved dismissal. "Never mind. Enjoy your weekend. My Mom will really appreciate it. And..." her voice drifted off.

"And what?"

"Oh..."

"What?"

"So is your girlfriend a movie star?"

"Nah, not my tribe."

I checked my phone for the time. "Hey, gotta run."

Not really, I knew, except having said so, something from the drug store? No. Better, I needed to work on my blog. I went to my room and faced the monitor. Nothing compelling came to mind, but a wisp of willpower forced me to drop into the chair and sign in for a look-see at my inbox. I clicked on New Message and began an aimless drift of words.

Togetherness, sort of

I wrote:

Holly: FYI, to clarify. My "girlfriend" and I are no longer in touch, other than an occasional e-mail. So if I go to LA this weekend, it will be to see my family. Tell your Mumsy to be careful around my stuff. The room is small and she could knock something over without meaning to.

In re-reading the letter, I labeled it pathetic.

But an unaccustomed need to explain myself lingered. I deleted that one and tried again:

Holly: You remind me of my mother. Her favorite saying is *Déjà de tamborilear con los dedos. Me estás volviendo loca.* Look it up. Or not. FYI, I played the drums for my high school band. Without sticks, my digits carry on to ward off evil. My heroes were members of the USC Trojans drumline. Look 'em up on YouTube. Or not.

I typed her name into the address line and punched SEND, then sat back and chastised myself for needing to clarify, especially revealing family triviality. What good could come of Holly knowing I drive my mother crazy? And nobody needs to know that working with drums can alter my disposition. If I could, right then, I'd beat the crap out of them.

No matter. After a few minutes, an answer arrived from the other bedroom:

"Carlos, FYI, I took a year of Spanish in school and understand two words, *no comprende*. Re: the USC drumline, wow! I played the piccolo in high school. Perfected "Yankee Doodle Dandy." The two of us would be sensational in a July 4 parade."

Surprise. Her positive tone rocketed my mood straight up. Plans swirled in my head. I'd grant Holly the reasonable favor of making myself scarce for one weekend, but not in LA. I'd use the time to catch up on reading in a hotel room, or better, check out the surrounding country here, maybe drive to Glen Campbell's Galveston to hear its sea winds blowin'.

Tangle of Secrets

Holly and I could continue our workable living arrangement in good spirits. For whatever it was worth, she'd take my actions as evidence there was no desperate female in LA longing for my body.

And the promise held—until the evening I ruined her birthday.

17

Ruined celebration

Professor Loder sent word suggesting a final visit to the dig the third week of September. He and his crew were about to wrap it up. Welcome news, because I was ready to move on to livelier subjects.

Following our routine, Holly left her car at *The Herald* garage and joined me in the van. We liked to compare notes during the drive.

"I'll give it one more blog, about the way Loder inspires his students," she said. "They're awed by him. How's your video working?"

"I shot a map of Texas dig sites and researched the cloning experiment." I'd been reading about Russian and South Korean scientists playing with DNA samples found in permafrost. "Now all I need is a summary," I said.

I didn't mention that Garon and the features editor had been hovering over all facets of my work and, short of diminishing their plausibility, heaped on the praise. I could only guess how my photo boss reacted. He continued to assign minor jobs to me, such as routine city hall stuff, but stayed too distant and preoccupied to comment on specifics. Could Blaisdale be resentful of the front office take-over of my work? Possibly, or he might simply be too busy going nuts. A couple of photogs who quit for industrial jobs would not be replaced.

Holly had seen the first part of my video for beginner science classes.

"It's neat the way you got the diggers to talk to little kids at their level. Their teachers are going to flip over it."

Her compliment got me going on a subject I hadn't verbalized. I told her I'd been pondering multimedia nature studies for kids. The dream kindled way back at my day camp experience with an upset little camper and a whispering tree. With technology leaping in all directions, the idea kept getting more complex and desirable. The thing about Holly is that she's a non-stop listener, which means that sometimes the talker, aka me, doesn't know when to quit. If it had been any other subject— world politics, religion, shopping—I wouldn't have much to say, but a nature course involving animated and narrated textbooks, even a TV show? Way to go.

"Give me an example," said Holly.

"Okay. I'm thinking about a lesson on evolution. For instance, some scientists have tapped into ancient genes and created giant versions of the species *pheidole morrisi*—ants with huge heads."

"I read about that. Won't that scare little kids?"

"More likely the other way around. I'll explain how the monsters protect the colony by using their heads to block the entrance of the nest.

"And that's only one idea. Camouflage, the way bugs hide from predators or adapt to other needs, or the ways in which humans mimic nature in their inventions—that kind of stuff is what I'm thinking."

With boundless enthusiasm, I pontificated, "News stories come and go. Those subjects hang on."

When I finally shut up, Holly took a deep breath. "Hmmm, yes. I can envision all sorts of possibilities."

Ruined celebration

I could almost see her creative wheels spinning, and it's good we arrived at the sand pit just then or her approval might have churned me up again.

Loder met us at the gate with the news that the find was about to be shipped off to the university.

"I'm going to haul equipment and bones up there in person," he said, pointing to a rented trailer. "We have the skull, about four feet of both tusks, and an amazing number of viable fragments."

Holly pressed him for his conclusions. She wanted a final statement about the woolly mammoth theory—was it now officially disproved?

"We've speculated, but the hair hasn't survived. That means it's probably a Columbian mammoth, the kind that adapted to a warmer climate. This old beast has been silent for a long, long time, 38,000 years, no less. We expect it to reveal all when a team of paleontologists has a go at it."

He assumed that once the experts have their say, the finds would be reconstructed and donated to a museum.

What would he do then?

He rubbed his sun-baked hands together.

"You think this baby is ancient? How about a dimetrodon? I'm going to join a crew digging in North Texas. They're finding bone shards that have accumulated 200 million years of dust. These old boys are finally telling their secrets."

"Exciting!" Holly glanced at me. "Carlos is planning a documentary for kids. Do you think they'd allow filming?"

"You bet. I'll give you a contact."

Great, but it was time to get busy. For once, at my strong hint, Holly had set up an assignment in late afternoon. It was still too early for the magic hour, the last one before sunset when light fades to a golden glow, but at least I wasn't dealing with harsh mid-day glare. A few sea clouds had rolled in, along with some acrobatic gulls, making my final shots even better for a dramatic wrap to the unexpected Gulf Coast discovery.

As we walked back to the van, Holly and I agreed that all the pieces seemed to fit. In both our versions, we had provided plenty of breaking news and educational links about the extinct beast. It might be extinct now, but some day crafty scientists may find a way to clone it.

I guess our thoughts groped in the same mist, because when we opened the van hatch to stash our stuff and leaned forward simultaneously, our heads collided. By accident. That's my story.

Holly rubbed her forehead and laughed. "My, how graceful."

I pressed my hand against her face. "You okay? Concussion or anything?"

She looked at me in a thoughtful new way, as if we might share something better than notes.

I caressed a thumb lightly over her sun-pinked cheek.

"You think?"

She contemplated. "Do I think what? Are you asking if we could be lovers?"

That was Holly—right to the point.

"Now that you mention it," I said, "we get along in lots of ways."

"True."

"Know what? I think about you at night, when you aren't there."

Her eyes filled with trust.

"You're so sweet, Carlos."

News photographers I've met so far display a range of dispositions. They may be arrogant, rude, dismissive, untidy, cool, brave, opinionated, suspicious, profane, and to be fair, warm and polite around crippled kids and old people. But sweet? Did she say sweet? Could I be the first in my line of work?

Her eyes reflected wonder.

Ruined celebration

"Weird, too." she said, "Usually I am there, only a few feet away."

"You mean I've been wasting my time?"

She brought a hand to my chest, a hesitant touch.

"Maybe. Or maybe it's best that way, not to rush, to know each other better."

The moment was a revelation for both of us. We let it glorify into a declaration, then, wonder of wonders, a gentle kiss. The time and place did not allow passion, just tender touching of mind and body.

It didn't last.

Suddenly she sprang back wide-eyed. A frantic sound came from her lips, something like "Aaackayah! Ack! Ack!"

"What? What?"

"Jeez! Something's looking out of your pocket. A big roach!"

I glanced downward to meet the beady peepers of a large brown-banded wing grasshopper *(orthoptera: Acrididae)*. Oh yeah, I had captured it at the dig, but forgot to pen it up in my camera bag. To complete its escape, the fine specimen spread its wings and took off with a loud, characteristic clicking noise, skimming right by Holly's ear. She squealed and dipped her knees, not exactly in sync with the speeding insect. I pulled her up and brushed her hair back.

"It's okay, baby, it's all right. It wasn't a roach, just a grasshopper."

"Did you say *just?*" Her voice pitched. Her hands clutched at her chest. "That thing was huge. And it had a motor!"

During the drive back, she demanded to know how I became so obsessed with insects. Was it parental neglect? Sibling rivalry? Delayed development?

"All of the above," I assured her. "The best photographers come from sordid and deranged backgrounds."

I remembered Garon's idea to give Holly some photo pointers, but she had acted a little touchy. Still, it seemed like a good time.

"Speaking of photography, a secret among news photographers is that today's cameras are smarter than we are. If lighting isn't a problem at a news event, we use the automatic setting."

She sighed. "Carlos, I don't know. I have so much else to think about. That aggregated blog they want me to do—it's no less a world round-up of related science news. That takes time."

"Right. But someday you could be in a situation without a photographer. In that case, you can look pro if you learn a couple of simple things."

"Such as?"

"Let's say you are using a current point-and-shoot camera and want to get a nice close-up of a sunflower for the garden editor. But there's a big garbage can in the background. You don't want it to stand out, so you blur the background. You set the mode dial to Av, then..."

"Wait. Why don't I just move the garbage can?"

"Uh, yeah, that could be an option. But I forgot to mention, the garbage can is crawling with squishy maggots and excited roaches and an emotional rat."

"Ee-ewww." She pondered. "Tell you what. I don't really need a picture of that stupid sunflower. I can find one on-line. Better yet, why don't I ask you to shoot it for me. Pretty please?"

"My pleasure, princess."

I saw no need to belabor the point. She might not accept cameras, but at least she approved of the photographer.

Our conversation took a few silly turns until she brought up a concern.

"I'll forgive you and your ghastly grasshopper if you'll remember that this is my birthday."

"Aw! Today? Are you sure?"

Ruined celebration

"Positive. Verified at 5:30 this morning. My mom calls me at that specific time on my birthday because that's when I woke her up twenty-four years ago. She tends to carry a grudge."

I offered Holly a lavish dinner out, but she said she didn't feel like dressing up. She'd rather get comfortable and cook a steak for us, then watch a movie she'd just bought.

"You can take me to Brennan's tomorrow night, okay?"

I liked the movie idea, picturing us cuddling on the sofa.

Back at *The Herald* garage where her car waited, we arranged an errand dance. She needed to hit the grocery store while I picked up my laundry. I made a couple of stops for a birthday card and a bakery something.

First to get home, I unloaded the stuff and went back to the mailboxes. Mine was a loser, only a catalog of cheap photo junk and a charity dun. Holly had a bonanza of birthday cards. Stacking them on the table, I glanced at the top letter. I read the return address once, twice, three times with stunned disbelief:

Foster Talent of Los Angeles, CA.

What the hell?

Like a zombie, I met her at the door, lifted a grocery sack from her arm, and listened to her banter about the favorites she planned to prepare in the Bryant manner.

"Birthdays in my family mean a home-cooked steak night," she said, unloading another bag at the kitchen counter. "And coffee ice cream. Hope you like the flavor. Do you?" She looked at me for a response, and saw trouble.

"What's wrong?"

"I just picked up the mail."

"Okay." She waited. "Not okay?"

"I don't want to be nosey, but there's a letter. Do you know Zack Foster?"

"Of course I do. Uncle Zack. Hope it's a birthday card. He always sweetens it with a check." She stopped. "Why are you staring?"

"I don't understand. If you have connections with Zack, why haven't you mentioned it?"

"What do you mean? You know all about it—he recommended you, same as he got me hired at *The Herald*. And why I felt comfortable asking you to room here. Didn't he tell you about me?"

"Not a word. I didn't know anything personal about you."

"You're kidding! It isn't a secret. He and Garon have been friends for years…

"I do know that."

"Thought so."

She emptied a grocery sack. "I try to do a good job so I don't disappoint either one. Particularly I don't want my uncle to have regrets. He's pretty careful about his endorsements. That's why Garon was so quick to hire you. Uncle Zack told him that although it would be a favor for his best friends, you were top notch and up on all the latest technology."

"What best friends?"

"Your parents. They asked him to…" her voice trailed off as if she were seeing an approaching disaster. She was right.

A wipe-out wave of anger enveloped me. It hit me with such suddenness I could only look beyond Holly while my thoughts sparked fire. *"They did it again. Again! Damn, damn, dammit!"* How humiliating to believe I'd earned a position at *The Herald* with solid credentials beyond Zack's recommendation, when all along it was another mommy-daddy set-up for babykins, a devious one at that. To double the embarrassment, I'd been pathetically ignorant about it while Holly knew it all along.

Fury! A new experience for me, like a car bomb in my head. A runaway pulse punched at my temples. The anger that flamed up

Ruined celebration

came mixed with resentment at all the controls and unanswered questions in my entire life.

"I'm not hungry," I said. I turned away with such force that I knocked a bag of groceries to the floor. Cursing under my breath, I scooped up stuff, dumped it on the table, and charged off. Holly stood in culinary limbo, and worse, in a shattered birthday celebration. I slammed my bedroom door like a kid in a tantrum. I dived onto the bed, unclipped my cell phone and punched my parents' number. What I planned to say was venomous and way overdue. *Let go of me. I'm not a kid anymore. I've had enough of your control. I'm sick of your constant interference. Back off. Do you understand? Back way the hell off!*

The maid answered in what sounded like a guarded voice. No, she said, the lady and gentleman were out for the evening. Would I care to leave a message? And then she asked, "Are you a relative?" Her question irritated me, and I hung up, dropping back against my pillow to glare at the ceiling until my pulse stopped galloping. Logic finally limped in.

Okay, if I wanted to come out ahead, I'd better take a wider view. It would help to know—finally—all the circumstances of my parents' actions. Why did they scheme to get me out of town? I'd settle for nothing less than a precise answer. That alone should convince them of my maturity. I let a few scenarios flicker through my head. Then, no, hold on. Did all that matter? I finally acknowledged a new, more important storm welling up inside me. If I was so in control, where did that infantile tantrum come from? Apology aside, how could I convince Holly that it was my first and last?

A car door slammed. I hit the floor and hurried to the living room window in time to see Holly's car back out and pull away. For no reason I could figure, a cop moving past flashed a light at the apartment, making a momentary sweep right into my face. Holly stopped at the corner, then turned left. The cop gunned a right toward downtown.

I imagined Holly was headed for some friend's place, female I hoped, where she'd make a bid for sympathy. She'd explain that her modest birthday celebration had been trashed by a raving idiot.

I stood there reviewing my stupidity until something else rolled over me. It took a minute to identify a deep, painful loss. Its intensity stunned me.

I needed Holly.

I wanted to hold her, to tell her I craved a big share of her future. A couple hours ago I had that chance—and blew it big-time.

Looking down at the miserable, dark street that lured her away, I wondered if she'd ever speak to me again.

The rest of the night turned out to be a burlesque of crossed paths. Battered by unaccustomed feelings, I elected a man-solution. I took off for the gym. A forced workout from hell might help me regain my adult senses. It did help, sort of like a vacuum cleaner sucking up brain dirt. When I got back, I saw signs that Holly had returned from another trip to the store. A bottle of wine sat on the dining table. She had opened Zack's card. A check for $200 lay on top of it.

There was no light under her bedroom door. Rehearsing my apology, I was about to discard unwritten rules and knock when my cell phone rang. The smallest hope swam in my head. Could it be that Holly heard me come in and decided to call?

No. Rotten luck, it was Photo with an assignment. A riot had broken out in the parking lot of a night club. The address was in a largely Hispanic part of town. It wasn't my shift, so why me? Oh yeah, my name is Montero. They think I'm fluent in Spanish. I grabbed my camera and took off. In the van, for old time's sake, I tried the alveolar trill once more: *sr-r-r-r-r-rpf, ur-r-rpfft*. Translation: *s-p-i-t*.

18

Bad news? No, the worst

The action was over before I got there, which is not uncommon in the news business. I pieced together a story about the riot by interviewing the cops and bar tender, checking for eyewitnesses on Twitter, and photographing a damaged car and trash in the street. Five injured, none seriously. Two arrests. Confiscated weapons. For Houston, a fairly quiet night. I sent raw photos and text to the paper and headed home.

By midnight, I silenced my phone and hit the bed. Next thing I knew, I heard Holly leave for the paper. Having worked the night shift, I saw no reason to rush. I took my time in the shower and kitchen—Holly had left the coffee plugged in. I filled a travel mug and headed downtown, parked, ambled toward the loading dock, pushed through the steel door, and rode the elevator to the editorial floor. Not until then did I wake up, and a rude awakening it was. Blaisdale charged through a door and accosted me with a high-pitched demand.

"Hey, why haven't you answered your phone? Garon has been calling for you. He's agitated about something."

"Okay," I said, trying to match his breathless tone.

I glanced at my phone, and sure enough, it showed a dozen missed calls.

Next, Holly popped out of a hallway and confronted me.

"Carlos! Garon is looking for you!"

"And I'm looking for you. I want to explain last night."

"Sterling idea, but not now." She grabbed my sleeve. "Come on, I want credit for your capture."

"What's going on?"

"I don't know. He wants to see me, too."

By this time, we were at Garon's door. She barged in with me in tow.

"I found him," she announced.

Garon stood up.

"Finally." He sounded relieved. "Carlos, sit down. You, too, Holly."

He removed his thick glasses and faced me with eyes diminished from owl to sparrow. I hadn't seen him so solemn, even pained.

"Zack Foster has been trying to reach you, Carlos. Your father was in a car wreck. He's in the hospital. Your family wants you to come home immediately."

A chill surged upward from my chest. I heard Holly gasp.

"How bad?" My voice seemed to come from another room.

"I understand it's serious. Zack says he went off the road in one of his antique cars. Rolled down a cliff and smacked into a boulder. Otherwise he would have gone down the entire mountain."

"Jesus, no!"

Responding to my shock, he tried to console me. "Doctors do magic these days, so don't give up. I expect you to catch a flight out as soon as possible. And Holly, I want you to go along."

"You do? I don't understand."

"Your uncle has some important things to discuss with you. The trip's on him. Personnel says you have a week's vacation coming and the archeological assignment is finished, isn't it?"

Bewildered, she said it was and started to ask questions, but he

Bad news? No, the worst

continued. "So under the circumstances, you can accompany Carlos and keep his spirits up."

She nodded—with some hesitation, I noted.

"All right, now you two need to get going. The business department is making your travel arrangements. Oh yes," he said to me, reaching for his notepad. He ripped off the top sheet. "Here's the hospital room number. Your mother is waiting to hear from you."

Shaken, I stood to leave. Garon extended his hand and wished me the best. I could only nod thank-you. My thoughts were already in Los Angeles hovering over my dying parent. *God, Pops, don't leave us. Please!*

Back in the hallway, Holly offered her sympathy.

"About me going, I can't believe it's happening, or why."

Odd, certainly, but that wasn't what I wanted to talk about.

"Holly, I'm sorry about my stupidity last night."

She ignored my apology to address the stupidity part.

"You went off like a rocket."

"I lost it, but it seems pointless now. Except for…"

"For what?"

"When you left, I missed you. I went to the gym and looked for a machine that would kick me."

"You should have asked me."

It struck her then that she was adding to my distress.

"Never mind. I don't want to discuss it now. Come on, let's hurry. We have packing to do."

19

No lovespeak

A fellow who had been sitting across from Holly helped her retrieve her luggage from the overhead bin. She joined the flow of departing passengers.

We finally reunited inside the LAX building.

"What happens now?" she asked. "I don't see Uncle Zack."

"Don't worry. We'll make connections. I need to go straight to the hospital, so come along. You don't have to visit my father. Just hang out in a coffee shop while I see what's going on, okay?"

She didn't look at all pleased, and I couldn't blame her. Where the hell was Zack?

Just then we were saved by a voice from down the walkway.

"Hey, little brother!"

It was Alex, grinning and waving.

If I had to put a number to it, I'd say Alex still rates as my number one favorite sibling, despite his enviable shrewd smarts as opposed to my more specific capabilities. He's not as tall as me, has good muscle tone, unflagging energy and a wardrobe of shirts I like to plunder. It wasn't enough to shake hands with Holly. Only a hug would do. I got a brotherly back-slap. He scooped up Holly's carry-on and, learning we could skip baggage, led us to the parking garage, meanwhile assuring us that Pops was holding on.

"I'm going to drop you off at the hospital and pick up Mama there. She needs a break," he said. "Zack is on the road, about an hour out. He wants me to take charge of you, Holly, so if you don't mind, I'll deliver you and Mama to the house. She'll enjoy your company, okay? And Carlos, Maggie is driving your wheels to the hospital, so you'll have your own transportation." He explained to Holly: "Maggie's my wife. You two beautiful ladies have Texas in common. I rescued her just in time from a miserable cotton farm down there. It was pitiful, boll weevils and mice everywhere. You could hear them gnawing."

I laughed.

"Don't listen to him. Hold out for Maggie's version."

Alex wears Pops' impish smile. I could tell by Holly's reaction that she didn't mind his nonsense, and neither did I. We kept the frivolity going until we pulled up to the hospital, where our moods changed to match the grim mission.

Maggie saw us approach the elevator lobby. She and Mama had been waiting on a bench and now stood for greetings and introduction to Holly.

It's interesting to watch women size each other up with polite little remarks. After Mama gave me a funereal hug to convey her pain, she turned to Holly and cooed, "What a pretty girl. Your Uncle Zack is so proud of you. I hear you'll visit with me for a bit and I am so pleased."

Holly said the expected things, how nice to be invited "but don't go to any trouble". Thirty-something Maggie, blonde and a reason for slender jeans, established eager kinship by shaking the hand of a "fellow Texan". Holly expressed concern for the suffering patient upstairs and learned that all the Monteros, Carmela, Juanita, and even Ricardo, were taking turns at the bedside, and without that kind of emotional support, Mama would surely be sick herself.

No lovespeak

Mama outlined the plan. After visiting Pops, she said, I would pick up Holly at the house and drive her to Zack's office. But before then, Mama and her guest would relax a spell, maybe have a restful tour of the house and garden, and then Holly could go to my room to freshen up if she liked.

Who said what melded to a cacophonous buzz. I sensed that, despite all the new faces, Holly made the grade and for the next couple of hours she wouldn't have time to miss Uncle Zack. In the way she avoided my eyes, she certainly wouldn't be missing me.

Alex and I stood mute until he rested a hand on my shoulder.

"He's in room 642. Guess you'd better go on up."

That alerted Maggie. She reached into her purse.

"Hon, here are your keys. Second level, third slot to your right. The tank is full. No new dents."

I stepped into the elevator and said all my goodbyes with a single wave. The foursome turned toward me in group commiseration for the duty I faced, and I appreciated their unified concern, but I also thought they looked cartoonish. It would have made a great shot if the elevator doors hadn't closed.

20

A need to know

I checked in at the station on sixth floor where a nurse waddled toward me.

"Your father is a pistol," she said. "He's been out of sorts all day. He keeps asking me two things, if I'm trying to kill him, and if you're here yet."

Inside the room, she motioned me to hold back while she checked his IV. I heard Pops cry out:

"Don't touch me! How many people have you killed today?"

"Now, now, Mr. Montero, if you talk that way, I'm not going to let you see Carlos."

"Carlos? Where is he?"

"Hey, Pops." I moved close to his bed.

"Finally, you're here. Woman, take your artillery and leave us alone."

"I will if you ask nice."

"If I could bend my knees, I'd get down and beg."

"Darlin', I live for your sweet talk." She swayed out of the room.

Pops grasped my hand as best he could. His vacant eyes watered, which I imagined reflected the pain of a broken arm, both ankles and god knows what else. Stitches on his forehead tracked into his graying hair, and one cheek bore a mean, puffy bruise. The bombastic one-time actor had been recast to a shattered invalid. He took the moment as a cue:

"Son, I am turning the last page on my life. All my days will soon share the same space as the most remote piece of history."

I couldn't think of a reply.

After an awkward silence, he gave up on me and ditched the drama to ask,

"How are you, Carlos?"

"Okay. At least I still have my ass, and I hear there's some question about yours."

"Protect it with your life. Mine has a hematoma. It feels like a pool of blood squeezing between my skin and the rest of me. Son, we've missed you."

I couldn't be sure his near-whisper was heartfelt. If true, then why had he arranged for my departure? But I buried the thought.

"You're one lucky guy, Pops. Was there mountain fog, or what happened?"

"I haven't told anyone yet," he said, showing some strength.

"Tell me."

"Well, dammit, the steering wheel came off in my hands."

"Oh, man!"

"I feel terrible."

"What do you need? The nurse?"

"Lord, no. Just some water."

I held the glass next to his quivering jaw, then grabbled a patch of his faded hospital sleeve to dab at a little stream trickling down his chain.

"What I meant, I feel rotten wrecking that fine old flivver, my grandfather's, you know."

I waited, fearful he might die then and there of a broken heart. Finally, he nodded.

A need to know

"Now son, I have something very important to tell you, in case this should be my death bed."

"Let's see, you're going to confess you killed somebody."

I meant it as a trivial remark, not a betrayal of my one-time fantasy.

"Killed somebody?" The idea bewildered him. "Well, it might have solved some problems," he said, managing a wan smile. "Do you remember my movie, 'Forever West?'"

"You laid it on me several times—the one where Zack Foster had a bit part?" I expected him to haul the yarn out one more time, and so he did.

"Yes, in a battle scene with a lot of extras. He played an infantryman and I was an Apache warrior. I got to sink a tomahawk into his skull. His acting career was over in less than a minute, a godsend for the paying public."

The memory twinkled in his eyes. Out of respect, I did not mention that in his earlier version, it was a well-aimed arrow, not a tomahawk. I watched the lighter moment fade. He sank deeper into his pillow.

"No, Son, this is not a joke. This is why I asked you to come home." His eyes focused on the ceiling as if he might find courage there. Finally he looked at me.

"Something happened years ago, Carlos, something you need to know. I do have a confession to make, especially to you."

21

Truth at last

Pops slipped his hand away from mine and absently rubbed his chest while searching the ceiling for words he needed.

Sit down," he said. "If I don't make sense, they give me drugs for pain, you know."

"I hope so, Pops."

Weak though it was, his theatrics survived.

"Years ago," he said, "I was about to make a breakthrough movie. I call it that because I wouldn't be playing a stereotypical blood-thirsty Indian. For a change, my contract looked good."

Stalling, he groped for a box resting on his bed. I retrieved it and held it while he extracted a small moisture pad. He dabbed at his parched lips.

"My co-star was to be a gorgeous young girl whose stage name was Estella."

Here it comes, I thought.

"We went into rehearsal. We said our lines; we danced; we embraced, all according to the script. She taught me some fancy steps. The setting was Rio, wonderful music and color, all created there on the lot. Good script, respected director. I had some funny lines. You wouldn't believe the advance publicity, thanks always to Zack. It couldn't have failed."

His thoughts turned inward to struggle with the next sentence. "But it failed miserably," he said finally. "And I was the culprit."

"What do you mean?"

"I mean I sinned against my loving wife."

"You had an affair? With Estella?"

"Yes, Estella. For a while, we knew each other too well."

He turned his head to the wall. I had never seen him look so unscripted. When he regained enough composure to continue, his eyelids fluttered against tears.

"Carlos, you were the result. You are my son, but not Mama's."

In an instant, the room's color drained. Stunned, I left the chair and moved to the window. Far below, cars crawled on the street in a silent gray stream, coming and going from private worlds. All of a sudden, everybody I knew was somebody else, including me.

I once had invented a potent scenario about my birth, thanks to Ricardo's dumpster story. But after I let my imagination exhaust the idea, I dismissed it. Now, answers to dozens of questions swarmed into my head. So that's why my charming brother bullied me. He knew. He dared not tell me outright, instead choosing to taunt me about safer details. And on that subject, Pops made everything right by attributing my green eyes to my mother. It wasn't a lie. He simply did not specify which mother.

"Son?" Pops coughed and groaned.

His distress upset me. I froze, even at the idea of ringing for a nurse. If I was aware of anything, it was that my hands were ice cold. I waited motionless until Pop's breathing calmed.

He begged, "Come sit down, Carlos. My voice isn't so good anymore."

I dragged back to the visitor's chair and sat with arms crossed.

"So where is she now?"

"She's always been nearby. She's always been a threat to us. But I couldn't explain that without telling you what happened back then."

"I know about her disappearance from the set, and about the scandal."

That shocked him.

"You do? How?"

"And you and the police. They questioned you several times. It's all in the archives."

"I don't know why you wanted to read that trash."

"What was your alibi?"

"Innocence. The truth would have been a worse scandal. She was intimidated by her bosses. She didn't want any part of Hollywood after she discovered it was anything but glamorous. The movie producer expected more than acting. She cried in my presence. Then, when it happened..."

"When what happened?"

"I already told you. I lost my senses. She was so beautiful and helpless, and she, well, afterward she just wanted out. I believed she was near a break-down. Zack and I arranged for her disappearance."

"Zack again. Then what?"

He started to reprimand me for disparaging his friend, but let it pass.

"He took her north to a convent where you were born."

"What about Mama? How did you handle that?"

"I've always adored Irma. God only knows why I thought it would be all right to cheat on her. If you need the truth, I wasn't thinking anywhere except below the belt. Then when Estella disappeared, all hell broke out with the press and the police. And of course, Irma had some burning questions. I confessed my sin and begged her to forgive me."

The memory played on his face, etching fresh pain.

"It was a bad time for us, our marriage. She let me know exactly how much I had hurt her. Every day was blistering hell. I had no defense. Crawling wasn't low enough. She threatened to take the children and leave me. The last thing I wanted was a divorce, yet… well, it got to the point where it sounded like the best idea."

He closed his eyes and shook his head as if to ward off the fresh stings of old memories.

"Finally, we both went to the church for counseling," he said. "We revealed everything. I told the priest what I had heard from Zack, that the young woman was emotionally unfit as a mother. She planned to give the child to the nuns. They'd find it a good home. I hoped somehow that would give Irma a thread of satisfaction."

Having passed the hardest part of his confession now, Pops found energy for the rest.

"The priest stayed calm and that was a help. If he had started preaching about sin and damnation, I would have walked out because my nerves were shot. If I was going to Hell, I didn't need him. I could get there by myself. But he did his job. He convinced us that out of mistakes come new beginnings. That's a cliché, isn't it? We were desperate enough to give it some credence. Even so, what he finally suggested sent Irma into another fit of sobbing and praying."

Pops heaved a sigh. I sensed he had control of the story and wasn't above injecting drama.

"The priest knew we had raised four wonderful children, and he suggested we take the baby into our own arms. After all, I was the father. He said Irma would learn to love the child just as if it were her own, another blessing from our merciful Lord. She could save the babe from an uncertain future."

He dabbed his lips.

Without looking at me, he said, "I can tell you, son, the next few weeks belonged to the Devil himself. I'd catch Irma glaring at me. Then she'd rush to the bedroom for a bawl. Then she'd disappear into the garden and whack at the hedge until it was just a stub."

At this point in his story, I got the clear and uncomfortable message that Mama hated me before I was born.

"But she kept going to church," he said, "and the priest won out."

Pops went on to explain that Mama accepted the idea with tight stipulations. Estella had to keep her distance. She would not be allowed to see her baby, ever. She was never to interfere with its upbringing. Above all, she could never reveal the transaction.

"It had to be kept under wraps because the slimeball gossip press kept watching our every move. Christ Almighty, they'd been climbing over our fence and looking in the windows. They even suggested I had harmed Estella."

I let him rest a bit before I prodded him:

"So tell me, how did you blackmail Estella to keep your reputation pure?"

"Son, I know this is hard on you, yes, of course. But just listen and then judge me, all right?"

I couldn't give him the satisfaction of sympathy. I could only shrug a cold agreement.

"Irma and I visited the convent the day before you were born. Irma stayed in the waiting room while I explained our idea to Estella, which was to raise you. In exchange, I'd support her for life. No visitation, no contact with us, even by phone, no formal custody papers—we didn't want to take a chance on notoriety. I made her vow absolute secrecy."

He took his time dabbing his lips for the third time.

"I had been working hard in the new business, putting some decent texture to the Montero reputation. Interest in the scandal was fading at last. Zack had arranged a luncheon with one of the flacks and dropped a rumor that Estella's father had come up from South America to drag her home. Estella agreed to the plan, with the understanding that if she slipped up, if the press recognized her, the money would be canceled. I arranged the payments so that Zack was, what would you say, a sort of money launderer? It would never be seen on the books. The monthly payment has always been taxed, always gone to Zack for professional services as my agent and again, when paid to her in her family name for so-called consulting services."

His eyes closed. He went silent for a spell. I had to bring him back with a question:

"Didn't anyone ask how Mama produced a baby in a single day?"

"Oh, yes. When anyone important to us asked, your Mama made up a little story, that one of her young unmarried relatives had been indiscreet, and that she was thrilled to volunteer as a mother. It would explain the family resemblance. As for the relatives, we simply said we had adopted you from an overburdened family. I don't believe any of them cared. Babies on Mama's side are a dime a dozen."

It's weird, finding out you aren't really you. Really weird.

Again, we fell silent. I needed to edit my perceptions of the past—not just mine, but of everyone in the family, and of many events over my life. The pause gave me time to realize that for years, beneath her shell of charm and community outreach, Mama carried a burden of suspicion and resentment.

Pops stretched for his glass of water. I got it instead and held it to his lips. The interlude moved us on.

"Okay," I said, "explain Estella. She hasn't been entirely out of sight, right? What gives?"

The subject stirred new anxiety.

"Well, that's another part of the story. Her instability never cleared up entirely. Everything worked at first, but during your early years, she hooked up with some guy who had money, meaning she had more clout. She would show up at Zack's office and demand to know things. Like what school you were attending. Then she'd go there so she could catch sight of you."

Before Pops went on, he tried to change his position in bed. He gave up with a grimace. It took a while to regain his voice, time I used to feel creeped out by the idea of having been stalked.

"Zack yielded to her because he thought she'd talk," he said. "That would expose all his own creative publicity back then, all that made-up stuff. Since you read the old papers, I guess you saw his baloney about her prominent South American family. So when she went on one of those look-sees, he always stayed close by to keep her from snatching you and maybe even claiming that we were the kidnappers. Zack and I still argue about his leniency. I accuse him of …oh, well." He let that thought sink. A sigh pulled in enough strength to continue with a potent account:

"When you were in the hospital, you know, the time you jumped off the balcony and damn near killed yourself, Irma waited until you were asleep and left the room for a minute to get a snack, and while she was gone, a woman slipped in. She was dressed in a nurse's uniform. Somehow she got you into a wheelchair and was already headed out the door when Irma came back. The woman panicked and ran off. She wasn't caught, but we knew. The hospital wanted us to report it to the police, but of course, we declined.

"Sure enough, lately Estella's gotten even bolder. She's a mature woman now, not a bit shy. And you aren't a kid anymore. She sees no reason for us to deny her a mother-son relationship. She insists on meeting you. And especially since I seem to be on my last leg, I agreed, so long as she continues to be discreet about it."

Last night's anger boiled up again.

"I wish you had asked me," I said, louder than necessary. "I want to know why you and your wife felt you had to keep all this a big, fat secret. You've always manipulated every minute of my life. Even sneaking me off to Texas, for god's sake. why?"

That stirred him up.

"My wife is your genuine mother, Carlos, give her that. From the first day, she has treated you as her own. Her maternal instinct fired up exactly the way it did for our other babies. And let me tell you something..."

"What?"

"She's nearly sick with worry now. She understands the logic of this meeting, that you are certainly old enough to handle it. But she's afraid you'll consider her pale next to Estella. Irma has always been terrified that she'd lose you, not just physically but emotionally. And me, I suppose. But I've kept my distance from Estella. Zack handles everything."

I had a sudden recall of the day camp years ago when the lady in big sunglasses drove up and took my picture. Her precise facial features long ago left my memory, but I've never forgotten Mama's tense reaction when I told her. The kidnapping scares made sense now.

I dreaded the answer to my next question:

"Okay, okay. So when is this momentous meeting supposed to happen?"

Pops glanced at the wall clock.

"Later this evening at Zack's office. He's driving her into the city this afternoon. By the way, Zack's wife doesn't know any of this either. We kept it close."

Pops again tried to deal with his battered body, but settled for letting me lower the bed and rearrange his pillow. I straightened the sheet and cover.

"Feel okay?"

"Tired. Terribly tired."

"Confessions will do that. Better get some rest."

"Good advice. Carlos?"

"Yes?"

Truth at last

"Never doubt that you are loved, son."

It was less a warm declaration than one of his familiar and firm directions.

"Sure, thanks. You, too."

"Remember now, call Zack. He's waiting to hear from you."

Delayed sympathy swept over me when Pops closed his eyes. That damned car really messed him up. He looked lighter, smaller in the bed—a result of spilling decades of guilt? Watching his frown lines relax, I realized the little kid in me wasn't scared of him anymore. His avalanche of information had shoved aside those restraints, leaving me with freedom and courage to ask him anything. Was I still mad as hell? No decision there yet. Too much was still happening.

A different nurse padded in to check the IV. I searched her eyes for information. She gave me a nod and a semi-smile.

"Everything's real good," she whispered. "Blood pressure's down."

I gave Pops' shoulder a farewell touch, hoisted on my backpack, and started to leave the room when he called.

"Carlos?"

"Yes?"

"In old age, son, there comes a time when everyone can get along just fine without you. It means you have done your job, you can take the off-ramp."

His scrunched up smile gave him away before I could argue.

"I haven't received that revelation yet," he said. "So I'll have to stick around."

"Yeah, Pops, you do that," I said, trying to return his smile. "Mama needs you back home."

He gave me a stiff wrist-wave of dismissal and, unless I misjudged, of triumph over a cloud of anxieties.

I left the room with my own muddled list. At the top was that call to Zack, which I likened to getting shots, nausea, dead batteries, flat tires, rejection slips, speeding tickets, and jock itch. Why couldn't I have just one mother like everybody else? Some days even one is too damn much. It would be nice to have a mature and level relationship with Mama, free of all her fretting. It was as if she spent her days dragging a dozen mean dogs clamped to her hemline, each one representing an imagined threat.

I paid the garage fee and reluctantly pulled out into familiar territory.

The palms, the sounds, the vibrancy, the showy pulse that is Los Angeles seeped back into my consciousness. None lightened my mood. What would happen if I dropped into a bar and sat it out instead of following orders? Why not? I'd been abandoned once, and that reminded me. Now that the dumpster story was disproved, it meant my parents had sent the wrong kid to the psychiatrist. It should have been Ricardo-The-Premier-Asshole. Or not. I'd have to admit that Ricardo had been a nonentity in my life lately, probably because we were on different paths. He was firming a career in Cabo with a luxury building project, while I was somewhere between this, that, and nowhere.

My thinking corroded steadily until I passed my longtime gym. I made an abrupt turn and drove back. A shower! Water to hammer down my befuddled head, to wash away the whole frigging day, to reconfigure me for the mystery encounter ahead.

Maybe not all that, but it helped.

When I arrived at the house, I remembered this was to be Holly's extended birthday. She hadn't mentioned it again, meaning she was still distancing herself. By now, she had spent time with Mama, and—damn, another realization—she'd be trying to freshen up in my room with the framed insect specimens and photos crowding every wall.

I called her cell.

"Holly?"

Truth at last

"Oh, you. I was hoping for an exterminator."

"Yeah, sorry about that. Hey, I've finished at the hospital, heading for Zack's office. You ready?

"Yes. Get me out of here. Where are you?"

"I'm pulling into the driveway. Come on down."

She stepped out on the balcony long enough to acknowledge me with a wave of her phone.

I made room by moving my backpack to the trunk. Minutes later, she slipped in beside me, bringing a perfume of bath soap. A fleeting mental image of her naked in my shower was the best thought I'd had all day. Immediately my old friend, the Guardian Angel of Shitheads, stomped on it.

"How's your dad?" she asked as we headed toward the gate.

"Better, maybe." I tried to measure her mood. "And you? Did you get the grand tour?"

"I did. Why didn't you tell me you were of the manor born? That's a huge house."

"Actually, I wasn't."

"Meaning?"

Stalling for an answer, I asked if she wanted the top up or down, and I deserved the look she gave me. The temperature was around 60 degrees.

"Ah, meaning?"

She wasn't going to drop the subject.

"Holly, there are some things I should tell you, if you haven't heard them from your omnipotent uncle. Has he mentioned Estella?"

"Who?"

Curiosity peeked through her peevish disposition.

"It seems I have some important business with Zack and a stranger, a woman named Estella. She's an old friend of my father's. And she just happens to be my real mother."

"Whoa, you mean the nice mother I've just been visiting isn't the only one? You have a spare?"

"You got it. But like I said, I'll have more to tell later."

Not at all subtle, I changed the subject by pointing out a couple of tourist attractions.

She pretended to be interested.

22

Behind a door

Zack's office is a low stucco building identified with sweeping script: "Foster Talent." I parked alongside and phoned to announce our arrival. When we approached the heavy glass door, there he was, dapper in a casual outfit of light grays to match his hair and moustache. He and Holly fell into a loving hug. Still holding her, Zack reached over to give me an enthusiastic handshake. He led us into his office, all the while scattering welcome chatter and a deep concern for my father, his best friend. Finally settled, he appealed to Holly.

"Sweetheart, I'd like you to wait here a bit. I'm going to take Carlos down the hall to meet someone. Get yourself a drink in my little fridge there." He gave her shoulder an affectionate squeeze. "I'm anxious to catch up on all the family news, and I have some, too. I won't be but a minute, all right?

"Go ahead," she said, already engrossed in his wall display. Row upon row of portraits and candids, a composite of Hollywood glamour, nudged each other. Centered high behind the ornate desk was a huge movie reel, still wound with its dated film.

"All right then." His tone turned serious. "This way, son."

That short walk down the hall felt like the last mile. This wasn't an assignment where I could hide behind a camera. This was a head-on reckoning of who I was, what was owed by and to whom. For sure, I wasn't ready for any kind of attachment. Way too late for that. As Zack reached for the door handle, I gave myself one guideline: Try to be reasonably polite.

Zack opened the door to a conference room. Hand lightly on my back, he ushered me in. The air presented a sudden change from bland to a subtle perfume. She had been waiting on the sofa. Now she stood and faced me with an expectant smile.

She was a stunner, maybe the best looking forty-something female I had ever seen—slim but curvy, wide-open green, *yes, green* eyes, soft taffy hair, scant make-up. Large hoop earrings flashed gold. A sparkling chain followed the neckline of a gauzy top. Trim ankles, spiked heels—no way could she have been the camp visitor. I had never seen this woman, never even in the photos of younger Estella, the dancer with exotic flowers perched in her jet hair.

In an instant, I forgave my father.

"Hello, Carlos," she said, her voice tender, expectant.

I wasn't through looking. What I finally said didn't come out right:

"Yeah. What took you so long?"

She hesitated, but her eyes held steady.

"The circumstances were never right—to say the least."

"So I'm told."

I searched for signs of kinship beyond the eyes. There was the slender nose, the rise of the cheekbones, lighter skin tone. Belying publicity shots I'd seen, this woman was not entirely Hispanic. It was evident that Hollywood had redesigned her with pots of makeup and a dark wig.

Zack spoke up.

Behind a door

"I'll let you two get acquainted while I keep my beautiful niece company. We'll be in my office. Take your time."

After the door closed, she gestured toward the sofa.

"Come sit with me. You must have questions. I don't know what they've told you."

She arranged her skirt and reached into a small tapestry bag for a cigarette. I found a silver lighter on the side table and scratched a flame.

"Thank you, Carlos—did you know I chose your name? I did, when they let me hold you for a few minutes. That was all I could give you. Then your father said he'd have to tell his wife it was his idea, or she'd change it."

Sorrow altered her voice. "Sometimes I was allowed to see you over the years, always from a distance. You never knew."

"Guess not—did you have an emissary one time? At a kids' camp?"

She brightened and reached into her handbag for a wallet.

"You mean when this picture was taken?"

There I was, a teen-ager framed by a car window, with tall timbers in the background.

"Who was she?"

"My longtime friend, Sister Mary Margaret. She had read the church bulletin and asked me if the nature photographer it mentioned could be you. She had a fine time plotting that venture. She said she even got some photography advice from you, all without any fibbing on her part."

Estella gave the snapshot an affectionate look.

"Oh, yes," she reminded herself. "I have something for you." She explored her dainty handbag and this time produced a wallet-sized photo of herself.

"I thought maybe you'd like to have it."

"That's cool, thanks," I said before testing her honesty. "Tell me, did you ever try to kidnap me?"

She averted her eyes.

"I was told to stay away, out of sight. They wouldn't even let me send you a birthday card."

"They? You mean Zack and my father, right?"

"None other."

"So, did you?"

"Try to understand how I felt, Carlos. I heard you had a terrible accident when you were a tyke. You were suffering in the hospital. It happened at a time when I was lonely, manic actually, and was feeling agonizing guilt for giving you up."

In re-living her failure, she held her hands in prayerful pose near her chin and stared past me.

"I was frantic," she said. "I dressed as a nurse and when Irma left the room, I went in. I saw a wheelchair in the room and thought I'd steal you away for a while, maybe take you for a ride in the hospital garden. I know, I wasn't rational in those days. I only wanted to talk to you, to see you up close. Getting you out of the bed was awkward, and I must have hurt you. When you began wailing, I panicked and ran."

"What happened then?"

"I didn't believe Irma saw me, but soon afterward I got a stern reprimand through Zack. Your father sent word that I had acted way out of line. So cruel!"

"So your next move was sort of a reverse blackmail, right?"

"It is not my nature to threaten. And believe me, I would have been extremely cautious about publicity. I didn't want exposure any more than your father did. But I thought if I upped the ante, it would convince him to give me a hearing. Instead, he tightened his demands. What I'm saying is, my schemes never worked. Irma was the holdout, of course. Until now, anyway. Frankly, I'm stunned that she agreed to this meeting. I guess she finally realized she can't hold on to you for your entire adult life."

"Have you ever met her?"

"Once, years ago, on the movie lot. She had her kids with her and didn't pay much attention to me. You might be interested to know that a couple of weeks ago I broke a rule and phoned her for the first time. I told her it was pointless and unfair to carry on the separation since you were grown now."

"What was her answer?"

"She was rude. She said she'd discuss it with your father. Then she hung up on me. I heard no more until after he had the accident."

"Where do you live?"

"Ventura. So near but so far."

"Never South America?"

She dismissed the idea with a dainty "pffff" sound and explained.

"Estella was a studio invention. You can thank your friend Zack for making me a Latina bombshell. The movie was to be a retro 1940s musical with a modern twist and some wild dancing. I had a lot of Puerto Rican friends from school and the neighborhood and I could do the moves and the accent. But I was just a puppy from Brooklyn, New York, USA. All those experienced people, the expectations—it was overwhelming."

"So how'd you wind up out here?"

What a series of lame interview questions, I thought—I really wanted to ask her about her affair with Pops and regrets for giving up her child.

"I impressed one of my teachers with my singing and dancing, and she put me in touch with Hollywood. She was with me for the audition, but had to leave after I won the role. I was on my own then, living in a small apartment. I was too young for all the obligations and attention, some of it quite personal. That's why your father…

well, he was older, and I trusted him. He was charming and kind to me. Carlos, don't think badly about him. I still love him."

I must have frowned. She was quick to amend:

"I mean for the way he took responsibility for you and how he has taken care of me financially all these years. My only problem was the unrealistic approach, the uncompromising rules he, or his wife, set down."

Rules, oh yes. Not only were we blood kin, we both experienced the Montero curb system. It was a strange connection, but I felt it nonetheless, along with a mild relaxation. I took a broad, less sensitive approach.

"So, in the interest of my genealogy, who were your parents?"

"Good question. I was raised in a foster home. I know my mother was Hispanic. She died when I was a babe. And my father was an Irishman of some sort. He was a poet and musician, I was told, but a drifter for sure. He vanished like an Irish wood sprite."

She laughed. "Never thought of it before, but I must have inherited that elusive elf gene."

I'm part Irish? Jeez, that's crazy, I thought. I'll have to send off for some clogs.

In the minutes that devoured themselves, she asked me about my life, my schools, my job and friends, especially the girl waiting for me in the office. Zack had told her his niece would arrive with me.

"Is something serious going on there?"

My answers were short, nonspecific, and considerate. I accepted that she needed to know these things. She appeared thirsty for every detail and quick with judgment.

"You shouldn't have moved away. Don't you miss your family?"

"Not really."

"Carlos, I don't believe you."

Behind a door

"Okay, I lied."

"Don't tell lies. They aren't worthy of you."

I resented her parenting, and changed the subject.

"Did you marry? Do I have a stepfather lurking somewhere?"

The question brought a scowl, but she answered.

"Yes, once. It didn't last and it doesn't bear mentioning."

"So you've been single all these years?"

"It depends on how you define single. I've had discreet relationships."

Her involuntary glance at the door gave a startling clue. Oh, my god, not Zack again!

About 45 heavy minutes into our conversation, Zack stuck his head in the doorway. "I hate to break this up," he said, "but the supers are about to lock the building."

It was done, the passage accomplished. Only it was strange how the solving of my life-long puzzle erased all traces of itself. It was as if the mystery had never existed.

We hugged loosely, politely, and I gave her over to Zack. Holly stood rigid to one side, giving Estella the once-over. I beckoned her close and introduced them.

"This is Holly, my Houston friend," I said. "And this is Estella."

She offered Holly a hand and a revelation for me.

"I am Martha Fitzgerald, darling. And I'm jealous of you for knowing my handsome son better than I do."

Holly managed a smile and the courteous standard, "I'm so pleased to meet you."

I had omitted "my mother" from the introduction. It could happen, given some reflection—and time.

In parting, the newly identified Martha touched my cheek.

"I love you, sweetheart," she said, her voice soft and maternal. "I have missed you so, all of your life."

23

Joyful confession

"I need food," Holly wailed. "A mound."

We were driving away from Zack's office, toward the house. Until Holly spoke, neither of us said much. My thoughts reeled under a double overload, my weird background, for one, but also a concern for Mama's state of mind. I pictured her solitary turmoil in the wake of all the revelations. She'd expect me to have some tough questions, and she'd be right. The questions would make us both uncomfortable, and I was tired of turmoil. I wanted to think about something else.

Holly's need helped.

"What kind of food?"

"A cheeseburger with bacon, lettuce, tomato, pickles and mayo, crinkly fries and medium mocha freeze. And a macadamia nut cookie. I crave triglycerides and cholesterol."

"Jeez. Watch for a drive-in."

We soon pulled up to a menu billboard. She draped over me to shout at a weathered speaker. A voice with a Doppler effect responded.

"Is that grrrsp-all-ll?"

"No. There's more."

We waited through an assault of static.

My turn.

"I'll have the same, but no cookie."

"No, no," said Holly right into my face. Her hand squeezed my upper arm the way Mama used to do when she demanded total attention.

"Yes cookie. If you don't want it, I do."

With our order completed, I eased the car forward to the service window—and to cool the sparks ignited by Holly's pressing body. An innocuous question might work.

"So how'd it go with Uncle Zack?"

"Way too interesting." She let go of me and sat back. "Our futures are in jeopardy. Yours and definitely mine."

"Ah, the rumored axe. Finally falling, is it?"

"True. As you know, he and Garon are like brothers, actually UT frat brothers. I've heard some wild stories. They tell each other everything. The word now is, *The Herald*'s sale is imminent. There's a big chance a veteran science writer from up East will fill my role. The reason Uncle Zack wanted to see me..." she glanced sideways to gauge my reaction "... was to offer a job."

"Doing what?"

"Publicity. Handle his celebs."

"Crap."

"Why not? He mentioned a super salary, and I'd be learning from a master, wouldn't I?"

Because I didn't answer, she filled in the silence.

"Uncle Zack doesn't get easy compliance from newspapers anymore. It isn't like the old days when you could walk right in without an appointment. That's a real downer for him. We talked about how today's papers are in trouble because they've shifted from news to selling advertising, and now advertisers are dancing with other

Joyful confession

partners. He sees his PR business turning more to social networking—that's where I'll fit in."

The service window whapped open. I traded bills for bulging sacks of steam and griddle smells. Instead of joining the traffic with the burden, I chose a parking space near picnic benches. We hauled our stuff out, spread it on a table, and sat side-by-side on the cleanest part of the bench. Holly's news further cratered my mood.

"This has been a helluva day, hasn't it?" I said. "We were going to celebrate your extended birthday tonight, remember? I was hoping to take you to dinner, buy you a little present, some flowers, I don't know what exactly. So here we are at a godforsaken burger joint. I wanted to do more."

"That's sweet. With all you've been through, I can't expect you to pay attention to my birthday. Anyway, it was yesterday. I'm already a day older. And wiser, for sure."

She was being considerate. Still, her new wisdom could never reveal the depth of my self-reproach, so I decided to plunge in with details.

"Holly, I know you're still upset and it bothers me. A lot."

"Well, yes. I've calmed down some, but I don't understand why you blew up last night. You nearly slammed the door off its hinges, and I can't imagine what set you off." She gave me a stern look. "We can't have much of a relationship if we can't communicate—like adults."

That was both exhilarating (a relationship!) and hurtful. I took a bite of hamburger and tasted remorse.

"Well?"

"I'm wondering if you need to know all my stuff. I try not to think about it myself."

Her paper sack rattled as she raked out little ketchups and mustards, straws and napkins.

"I'm listening."

"Okay."

Time passed.

"Still listening. Hearing nothing."

"I know, I know. I'm trying to begin."

She crunched into a pickle and grabbed a napkin. A drop of cold juice pinged my cheek.

There was no backing out. Because revealing personal matters had not been my style, I munched on my burger between sentences. Eventually she learned how unyielding my parents had been, how they expected me to take their actions for granted.

"I'm not whining," I told her. "I had a privileged upbringing, but I always felt hampered by rules made specifically for me, even in college. So in Houston, I finally tasted independence. An adult among adults. It was a terrific life change, Holly, not to mention meeting you. And then, wham, right there in your kitchen I learn it's all an illusion. And sure enough, I took it like a bratty kid. I'm embarrassed. I apologize."

Holly-the-listener's face turned solemn as she understood why her connection to Zack had ignited my bonfire. A blend of guilt and sympathy softened her eyes.

"I'm assuming your uncle explained the business about Estella, I mean Martha," I said.

"Not all of it."

The rest of the story came easier. I detailed the flawed suicide theory, the pointless psychiatric consultations, and even Ricardo's early strikes. I added, however, that distance and passing years settled our differences to the point where we didn't find each other especially interesting.

For most of my frustrations, I told her, I turned my attention to stuff I could control.

"Like chasing insects."

Joyful confession

"That and photography. Bugs make good little subjects. All they ask is a few stings and bites."

I gave her an earnest look. "But for you I can broaden the spectrum. How about birds and butterflies? Or warm puppies?"

She nodded.

"Puppies for sure," she said. "Yes, birds, yes butterflies. No military grasshoppers, please. And how about a suspension on beetles, especially the ones that eat dung—I saw one framed on your wall. Jeez."

In this promising moment, I tested her reaction.

"So back to my original point. Are you still angry?"

She concentrated on folding a paper napkin in her lap.

Not anymore, because…"

I saw the beginning of a smile.

"Because why?"

"Because I am in love with you, Carlos. And after you walked out last night, I've been miserable thinking you're not feeling the same way."

I let my staggering relief show in a silly grin.

"I changed my mind," I said.

"About what? About me?"

"No, about the cookie."

That almost got me a punch in the ribs, but I caught her dainty fist and drew it to my lips. She reacted by melting against my chest. Her hands found the back of my neck for an arousing caress. She was mine, pickles, fries, and all.

24

Arboreal solution

"Uh-oh." After pulling through the gate, I realized the set of keys I was using did not include one to the house. "How do you feel about spending the night in the car?"

"Carlos, baby, it's too cold for that."

"I'll keep you warm." I snuggled her close to me.

After our first real-in-every-sense kiss, she pulled back with a question.

"So, what did you decide?"

"I decided I love you."

"That's not what I meant."

"What then?"

"Are you moving back to Los Angeles? I mean, if I work here with Uncle Zack…"

"I need to discourage you. Chasing insecure show-offs is a waste of your talent."

"I see. That means you have a greater role for me, right?"

"Absolutely. I'll explain when we get inside."

"Fine. I like that, I guess. I'll try not to look at your bugs. But how are we going to get inside without a key? Like maybe ring the doorbell?"

"No way, we don't want to wake anybody."

I took advantage of the interlude by drawing her close again and whispering against her face.

"I want to make love to you."

"I don't think so."

"Why not?"

"We're sitting in the driveway in a convertible."

"I hadn't noticed. I'm blinded by passion."

"Too bad there isn't a separate way to your balcony. I left the doors open."

"You just solved the problem. Come on."

I closed the car doors quietly and led her to the green gem ficus tree, which stood tall and dignified by virtue of age and, in my history, by usefulness. Its thick blanched trunk and above-ground tentacles of roots captured moonlight like a fairy tale garden. Its sturdy white limbs pointed skyward in short distance from each other, and a couple of them nestled against the balcony's iron rail.

"You expect me to do what?" Holly's whisper defined wonder and disbelief.

"It's easy! I've done it hundreds of times. I'll hoist you up to the first limb. Then just step up to the next one. I'll be right behind you." That said, I grabbed her hips and raised her high. "Got it? Pull up!"

"Yikes, it's bouncing up and down. Will it break?"

"No, you're a lightweight. Just hang on." I watched her reach for the higher branch and inch upward from a seated position.

With a foot shoved against the trunk, I reached for the lowest limb and in one motion swooped up beside her.

"Now grab this one. I'll hold you."

She strained higher.

"What a novel use of time," she complained. "This morning I was sanely in my bed in Texas and tonight I'm in a tree in California."

Arboreal solution

"A reasonable progression. Lean a little and take hold of the next limb."

"What if there's some kind of nest? Like wasps or something!"

"They'll forgive you. One more limb. Good. Stretch your foot out and step on the edge of the balcony. Then ease over and grab the railing."

"I don't think so."

"Do it."

"Probably not."

"Please?"

"Ohmygod hold me tighter! If I fall and die, you have to go with me."

"I will, I promise. Reach for the rail. Okay, now your other foot."

"Yikes! We're so high up."

"Don't look down."

In a rustle of leaves, I was beside her. I arched over the rail for a soft landing.

"Where are you going? Don't leave me here!"

I leaned over and clasped her waist. "Hold on now, I'm going to lift you high. Yeah, let go of the tree and grab my shoulders. It's okay, let go."

"Not yet. Are you leaning against that rail? How strong is it?"

"Holly, listen to me. I will not drop you. Let go of the limb and reach for my neck. Okay, that's one arm. Now…"

"Mercy, something broke off."

"Bring it with you."

In her panic, she let go and moved her arm so abruptly that her bouquet of leaves slapped the back of my head. Her grip squeezed around my neck, and as I eased her over the rail, she fastened her knees like pliers against my legs

"Good girl! You did it!"

She gasped, "Maybe so, but my shoes didn't. They fell off."

"You won't need them."

25

Getting real

In my early years, I never discussed sexual stuff because I didn't want to reveal either my intense curiosity or my ignorance about a willing female body. I strained to listen to every detail when guys my age carried on. I did know all the textbook particulars, and one momentous night in his darkened bedroom, watched an explicit movie with Alex-the-Procurer who worried that I was late to bloom. Maybe so. So thanks to brother Alex, I advanced to dating in high school, a few sessions of heavy petting and—enter here the duh! factor—a midnight session with a seductive cutie I met at a party. Until she demanded cash, I had no idea she was a pro.

In college, I finally displayed subtle skills around females. When I'd emerge from solitary study into a bustle of human activity, I'd hang with a campus minority. We were fitness and bookish freaks—self-proclaimed intellectuals without the credentials—who avoided booze and instead OD'd at Starbucks to pontificate on lofty (read useless) subjects. Dating was casual, transitory. Affection, respect, but no strings—that was our cultural milieu. For us, sex was mostly a nod to nature, while binding love was an illusion. "Look at our parents," one of our jaded members said. "Who needs that?"

Tangle of Secrets

This business with Holly was different. By the time we conquered the tree, we'd been exposed to each others' temperaments and values. Besides appreciating her lively, no-frills good looks and intelligence, I admired her accomplishments, and she approved of mine. Reporters on routine assignments pair up with the available photographer, but I noticed a couple of times Holly changed an appointment to coincide with my schedule. We fell into an easy working partnership—except when she couldn't resist making photo suggestions. At least she waited until I finished shooting my way. We didn't exactly argue about anything, instead got into some discussions with furrowed brows and capitulations. If I challenged her opinion (rightfully), Holly-the-comedian had a way of lowering her chin and looking at me through eyes raised to the extreme, that look a bull gets when about to charge. Sometimes I'd give in. Others, I'd get the upper hand by threatening to snap her picture. She hated that.

I never guessed until the night in my room that she had dreamed of this moment. Why hadn't she signaled? Because I was from California, she said.

"I needed to observe you for a while, to see if we were the same species."

"And?"

"Close."

She dismissed restraints. Her hands drew my face toward her eager lips where I was burning to go.

What followed was so easy, so right. No more doubts. We were hot in love and we both knew this was not a one-nighter. Every touch, every word we spoke forecast endless paths ahead to explore. I didn't ask Holly if she'd marry me. I asked her when. Her answer made perfect sense in my possessed state.

Getting real

"Right this minute," she said. "I'm not going to let you get away."

At dawn, when we awakened in each other's arms for more tenderness, I encountered an old truth: Bonding empowers a man with positive forces. When I was a kid, I had embraced a hero, Super Big Guy, without understanding that he represented my ideal adult. Now I realized I had invented myself. Not that I'd be soaring off any more balconies, but thanks to Holly, I was soaring far above the events of the last 24 hours. I'd be able to steady a course, whatever its impact.

At this point, it felt natural and necessary to imagine our combined future. Love-making and shop talk—crazy, but the combo of passions defined us.

Speaking our plans softly, we decided to stick with *The Herald* long enough to experience its shift. We might be the first to go, or be granted enough time to witness some of the lay-off parade. We'd bid farewell to friends in crisis, probably at a Coffee Grounds wake. A compassionate office ritual, yes, but Holly had a few unfeeling nominations and I threw in the toxic picture editor.

"You mean Sandra Richards? She's a nice woman," said Holly. "She's raising two kids and is taking care of a husband who got a brain injury in Iraq."

"Rats, you ruined her for me. Now I'll have to like her."

"Good. You heard about Rob Blaisdale, didn't you?"

"Did he finally crater?"

Quoting Uncle Zack, Holly told me Blaisdale was considering a job offer to shoot documentaries on international oil rigs. He'd be taking helicopter rides over treacherous seas, chasing oil spills, shooting energy moguls, all to illustrate oil company propaganda. A cool, relaxing job after *The Herald*. The idea amused us. We wished him success.

"And odd thing—a bunch will get canned at the Help Desk, so help us all. Uncle Zack couldn't remember Dennis' name, but he quoted Garon saying that the smartest one will stay on to run what's left of the department. That has to be Dennis," she said. "I hope he can handle it."

"What about William Garon?" I asked. There couldn't be many managing editor jobs available these days.

"I brought that up, too. Uncle Zack says Garon hasn't been prudent with his money, so he's thinking about buying a camper and just roaming around the country, dodging creditors."

We tried to adjust to that absurd picture, but decided it was Garon's cynical joke. A weekend rancher with an inherited spread in Central Texas, he'd more likely be driving his Cadillac pickup.

"To the bank," Holly concluded.

We tackled our own needs. As soon as I mentioned (yet again) leaving the news business to create a miulti-media nature program for kids, Holly appointed herself editor.

"It should be an aesthetic experience. Give 'em an appreciation for nature's tricks with color and design."

"That's a slew of subjects," I said. "We'll need to start with an outline covering the whole spectrum before we get into specifics."

"Yes, boss." She absorbed my ideas with quick nods and astute questions about publishing trends, which seem to change every day.

True, neither of us knew what we were facing, but our experience in journalism would make it easy to find contacts and sources. Anyway, we noted most successful adventures begin with a degree of ignorance, and that settled, we abandoned mental work for another session of caresses and lovers' mumbles.

"Okay, sweet thing," she said, entwining her fingers with mine "Uncle Zack is definitely off my radar, and you are on big-time, but there is a nagging problem. I may have to go to a shrink."

"Let me guess. Insect phobia?"

"Not really. I've downgraded my phobia to a mere aversion, and

Getting real

I'm working on that. I have a nasty pet roach now."

"You're kidding me."

"No, really, he stays in the garage. His name is Cocky."

I planted a congratulatory kiss on her cheek and told her how proud that made me.

"Well, thanks, but it's only a first step. Cocky is dead. I sprayed him."

"Damn, woman, what kind of pet is that? How will you teach Cocky to sit and stay?"

"Don't have to. He's already doing it."

I don't know why I remember that screwball exchange. For sure, love had plunged our intellects to grade school level. We carried on with silliness until I came to my senses and faced a solemn duty. It was time for an important discussion with the lady of the house before she made her daily hospital visit. Holly understood and agreed to take her time getting dressed.

The dynamics of the new Bryant-Montero team churned in my head. I headed downstairs in a trance, absently pulling on a T-shirt. I wondered if it might be a good idea to run our plans past a couple of agents in LA before we returned to Houston. Zack could be a help, or maybe…

Too soon, I was at the patio door with the task of facing the woman who just hours ago had lost a son.

26

A garden for choices

I found Mama outside. She stood as quiet as the garden mist, apparently distracted by thoughts other than the cut flowers and damp shears she held. She looked crisp in a blue suit with the sleeves of a white sweater looped loosely around her shoulders. Her lipstick was in place, but by unusual oversight, she hadn't quite tamed her hair-do. Otherwise, except for protective gloves and yard-friendly flats, she appeared ready for her session with Pops.

The crunch of gravel under my feet startled her. I was alarmed to see her swipe tears from her cheeks.

"What's the matter? Did the hospital call?"

"No, dear, I've talked with your father. Thank God, he's finally sounding more like himself, griping about the nurses. I'm going to take him some flowers."

She forced a smile. "I'm just tired, I guess. Not sleeping much these days."

"Guess not, but something else is bothering you, isn't it?" Getting no reply, I drilled on. "You know about his conversation with me. You know I met her, don't you?"

She looked away.

"We need to talk about it, Mama."

Tangle of Secrets

I tried not to sound tense or demanding. I guided her past the pool and a swath of electric magenta ice plants to the iron garden bench. We sat facing each other, momentarily searching for a beginning and perhaps an ending, a way to rename years of deception. Long accustomed to the secrecy, she could find no starting words, so I began.

"I don't want to upset you. It's just that I need to know some things."

She set aside the shears and let the flowers fall to her lap.

"Carlos, I saw no need to tell you, ever," she said. "You were my baby from the first day. I loved you too much to have it any other way."

"But didn't you overdo? I had to account for every minute of my time. I don't think you were that protective with the rest of your kids."

"I guarded all my children. But when you jumped off the balcony, I thought I would die."

"I didn't jump. I had a flight plan."

She dismissed my version.

"You hurt yourself terribly. And those things you wrote. You wanted to leave us. Carlos, you almost killed yourself. I never stopped worrying about you after that. You were different from the others, like, for heaven's sake, the way you even denied your name."

"What do you mean?"

"Don't you remember? You signed all your school papers with some strange word. You said it meant nine hundred, but that never made a bit of sense to me."

She was recalling my long-ago secret name, NONGENTI. I had to grin.

"You never figured that one out, did you? NONGENTI is Latin for 900. The way you write 900 in Roman numerals is CM."

"Get it?"

"Get what?"

"CM—my initials."

"Oh."

She allowed herself to feel foolish.

"Maybe sometimes I worried too much."

"Only every minute of the day. And night."

She took a defiant breath.

"I couldn't help it. And later you were a special challenge, the way you liked to sneak away with your friends in the middle of the night."

"Had to. You wouldn't have let me go."

Then I got to the real point, which we had been circumventing.

"What about Pops? Did you forgive him?"

The cold question stunned her, and she shrugged.

"A lot of women deal with that kind of thing. It's not so different."

"Yes, but they don't usually take in the other woman's baby."

I paused before jarring her with another one.

"Was there revenge involved maybe?"

Mama came undone. She trembled.

"No! She wasn't going to keep you. She was going to give you away to strangers. I couldn't let that happen. You were family, my husband's blood, and it would be shameful to think he would never see you again, that somebody from who-knows-where would take charge."

It was her version of the truth, less painful. I allowed her to avoid mention of the priest's dominant role, and of her torment, her initial refusal to accept his advice. Again, thinking how close I had come to being someone else made me feel odd, disconnected.

"Did Pops think that way? Or was he just feeling guilty?"

"Your father loves his children. You wouldn't remember, but when you were in the hospital, he cried real tears over you. He stayed by your side for hours. Oh yes, he wanted you and never regretted his decision. Many times he thanked me for mine. All these years he felt he did the proper thing, to support her in trade for you."

"And for her silence."

"He chose to take that chance."

I softened my voice, but kept it steady.

"You knew this day might come, didn't you? That you'd have to tell me I'm not your son?"

Suffering for an answer, she closed her eyes, lowered her head, and absently rubbed a leaf between her thumb and forefinger. Its pungent aroma drifted between us. The interval lasted too long. I could tell she was girding herself for rejection. When she finally raised her head and squared her shoulders, she spoke as if she had disassociated herself from all expectations.

"Carlos, I've been trying to adjust. I tell myself you are grown now and don't need me. It's so hard, though, to give up a child, no matter the age."

"That's what she's thinking too. You knew she's stalked me since I was a kid."

"I learned that long ago. I can almost understand what she's gone through. But now it's going to be the other way around."

"How so?"

"She's going to be—well, someday you'll have Emilio's grandchildren. They won't be mine."

I reached for her hand.

"Mama, stop that. I know it's odd at my age, but I'm going to talk to Alex about drawing up some adoption papers."

"Adoption? Who?"

"You're going to adopt me! I'm not letting anyone come between us."

It took her a moment to realize what I was thinking. Suddenly she bowed her head and clasped her hands, this time in reverence.

A garden for choices

She whispered:

"Oh dear God, thank you. You've granted a miracle."

Too heavy.

"I know what you've been praying for. It's not about me, is it?"

"What do you mean?"

"You just said it. You want a bunch of howling grandkids."

"Not right now. In time."

"Hey, Holly and I may have started one last night."

Mama's spine went rigid. She snatched a bunch of flowers and smacked them against my shoulder. Blossoms flew.

"Carlos! Shame! You aren't married!"

"Now look what you did! You broke their little necks. Pops will think you're bringing him weeds."

She surveyed the damage and a smile broke through.

"Think so? Serves him right."

"I hear you. Give him hell."

She beamed.

"That's not a bad idea either!" Brushing leaves from her lap gave her time to consider the practical. Her words came fast.

"Don't worry about adoption. It's only paper, something for the gossip columns. I just don't want to lose you."

She fastened stern eyes on me.

"Except to Holly. She's a sweet girl, Carlos. You'll be smart to marry her. And from what you tell me, the sooner the better."

"Great idea. Holly thinks so too. How about right here in your prize-winning garden?"

I was being funny, sort of.

"Oh-o-o…"

Her eyes sparkled.

My next move was spontaneous and necessary. I gathered her into a mighty hug and almost reverted to the neediness of childhood.

Tangle of Secrets

This woman had every right to hate me at first. Instead, she had turned on all the burners of maternal love. When I let her draw back, I saw happy tears and a tender smile. That's all it took to open the right door.

"I love you, *Mamacita*," I said. "Know what?"

"What?"

"That other woman doesn't count. She's a nice lady, I guess, but a stranger. You're my mother. I'm your son. Like always."

Happiness does glow. Watching her beam, I found freedom to expose my misdeed.

"Guess I'd better admit something."

She didn't look surprised.

"Oh? Now what?"

"I don't really live around the corner from a police substation. I just let you believe that to calm you down."

"I know. The nearest one is eight blocks from you, but it's all right. The officer promised he'd drive by your place every night."

She tracked down the substation? She gave orders to the Houston cops? They complied? Oh sure, somehow I knew that.

My burning anger of two nights ago? Ashes. Ancient history. Even the patrol car with the flashlight was okay.

Mama dismissed our confession trade-offs with the sudden realization she needed to rush inside and tidy up.

"I'll buy some flowers in the hospital gift shop," she called back, satisfied and triumphant.

As I watched her renewed spirit bound into the house, a vision engulfed me like a collapsed tent.

Oh my god, what have I started? She'll want to stun the world with a wedding extravaganza.

I raised my eyes in appeal for a highly dependable angel, not the low-ranking guardian type—I wanted attention from the head intermediary, the one with six wings and a rabbit's foot.

A garden for choices

Instead, I spotted movement in the hall of portraits upstairs. It was Holly, dressed in brights, and ready to go. Her hesitant wave asked if it was okay to interrupt. She got a sweeping all's-clear.

Holly soared down the stairs. Outside, her bare feet reacted tenderly to the walkway, but that didn't slow her. New sunshine frolicked in her hair and heightened her colors. She thumped against me.

"Gotcha! My very own photographer!"

Right. She owned me. It felt fantastic.

Done with secrets, we were off and running toward new goals—except as a useful beginning, we needed to rescue a pair of shoes somewhere under our accommodating green gem ficus tree. Sure enough, they were there but already found and placed neatly next to each other, toes pointed toward the balcony. I got the message: My loyal old friend Humberto was still watching, and probably laughing at my handling of love.

When I was a kid, pumped with imagination and emotion, I thought I could fly. It turned out I was right.—NONGENTI

Acknowledgments

This story owes much to editor Bonnie Britt of Berkeley, CA. A former colleague in news gathering, she persuades, cajoles, and lavishes encouragement until the job is done.

Made in the USA
Charleston, SC
08 August 2013